UNAFRAID

MEGAN LYNCH

CITY OWL
PRESS

UNAFRAID
Children of the Uprising, Book Two

CITY OWL PRESS
www.cityowlpress.com

Cover Design by Olivia at MiblArt. All stock photos licensed appropriately.

Edited by Amanda Roberts.

For information on subsidiary rights, please contact the publisher at info@cityowlpress.com.

Print Edition ISBN: 978-1-944728-76-2

Digital Edition ISBN: 978-1-944728-75-5

Printed in the United States of America

To my grandmother, Gay Fields,
who teaches love by her love.

CHAPTER ONE

DENVER RAY HUGGED HERSELF AGAINST THE HARSH JANUARY wind. Even with her head down, it lashed at her face and forced tears from her eyes. But after a long shift of cooking for two hundred people inside the dining room of the monastery, it wasn't unwelcome.

It was a good place—and they'd been here for the past six months—but it never resembled any sort of home, either. Much too cold. When they'd stumbled upon the evening singing, Bristol, Samara, Jude, Denver, and Stephen could hardly believe it. The mostly-torched sign at the end of the dirt road read *St Mary of the* — but what exactly she was the saint of was cut off, the edges of the wood singed by a long-ago fire. Bristol joked that it was St. Mary of the Hopeless and Defeated, but Stephen said that couldn't be right—after all, they were still alive.

Inside, hundreds of people were hiding from the relocation, in just the same situation they were in themselves. None of the incumbent members seemed surprised to see the new little family band of outlaws. Denver and the others were shown around and drilled in the rules of the monastery. They were told they would be moving on to Canada soon, but they would be traveling all together. Once you were here, they said, that was the only way to get out—together. That notion was as close to togetherness as it got here—the people finding refuge were not keen to make friends. And as far as Denver could tell from the way the leaders spoke to the big group of them, there was still no flight plan.

But it didn't matter. The exit from Nan's had taught them to be prepared, and they were. Denver and the others wore their backpacks under their coats and slept with their shoes on, ready to run at a moment's notice. No one else had asked about it, even though they had to be curious. She hadn't been asked about anything, except for food stock and storage, since she got here. No one else seemed as lucky as she'd been, being with her husband and finding her brother and his friends alive. She understood.

Denver frowned and looked at the ground. Was that frost? They lived in fear of snow here, as they had no way of covering their footprints, but the weather had been obliging so far. The leaders here were always hinting that they had some sort of plan worked out for all of these situations, but something inside her had cracked and broken—after a lifetime of trusting authority, she suddenly found it impossible to believe someone was looking out for her. Like a childish dream, though it'd seemed so real, it had vanished the moment she'd woken. There were only two people she could truly trust now—her husband, Stephen, and her brother, Bristol—and here, they were as powerless as she was.

The girl's dormitory was warmer, but only because of the lack of wind inside. Denver kept her coat on as she sat on her bed. She took off her shoes for a moment and massaged her feet. She'd been fantasizing of sitting down for hours. Samara, also tightly bundled in her winter wear, sat next to her.

"Are you still looking for something to read?" asked Samara. "I just finished this one."

Denver leaned over and took the book from Samara's mitten. "*Great Expectations*? What's this?"

"I think you'll love it. It's about a boy who—"

"No, thank you, then," said Denver. "I don't like boy books."

Samara frowned and took the book back. "Okay. I'll see if Jude wants to read it."

Samara walked away, and Denver leaned back against her thin pillow. Maybe this time she'd get the point. It wasn't that Denver didn't appreciate everything Samara had done to help—she was sure Jude wouldn't be here without her, and he was fine, she guessed—it was just that Bristol would have done just fine without Samara, and now that she was here, they were stuck with her. There were too many things about her that seemed suspect. Why would she put herself at risk to save a little prisoner boy? Why did she find it so easy to leave her parents, her job, her life in Metrics? Whatever she was hiding, Denver wasn't interested in becoming involved. *Once we get to Canada*, she thought, *we can get rid of her.*

She couldn't help thinking thoughts that began with "once we get to Canada." Denver prided herself on her pragmatism, and she knew that pessimism and suspicion would not serve her on this issue. For the sake of her sanity, she had to believe they were getting to Canada one day.

Denver closed her eyes and dug her thumbs into the arch of her foot. There was a rhythmic knock at the door, and Denver slid her shoes back on to go answer it.

Bristol stood on the little stoop with his hands wrapped around a thermos. Denver pulled the top of her coat around her throat. "Are you here to see me or her?"

Bristol seemed to miss any leftover resentment in Denver's tone. He smiled and leaned in. "You. I got some hot cocoa."

"Shh!" Denver stepped outside and closed the door behind her. "Where?"

"I'll tell you in a second. Let's go to the Spot."

The Spot was actually a tiny chapel in the valley. It was one of the unspoken places where people could go to have a private conversation, and it was truly amazing how well it was respected. If someone else was in the Spot when you wanted to go, you just walked around until it was empty again. There was no scheduling, but no fighting over it either. The ten-by-ten cinderblock room with a wide table along one wall was always clean, though many seemed to use it for what might be called dirty activities. Denver had been there with Stephen more than once.

Today, she and Bristol sat on the outside of it, on what would have been the sunny side if the sun had been out. The wind knocked against the opposite side and whistled around them. Bristol poured some cocoa into the cup and handed it to Denver, who wrapped her hands around the sides. Bristol did the same with the thermos. "It's not really a secret or anything. It's a reward for being a good little boy."

"You found something on watch today?"

Bristol nodded. "I don't think it's significant. I just saw Metrics patrol pull a car over."

"What color?"

"Red."

Denver lowered the cup and locked her eyes on her brother's. "Then of course it's significant."

Red was how they recognized fellow runaways traveling along their path: the Red Sea. The group itself was loose and unofficial, but there were unwritten and widely-known rules. One was that anyone traveling in a transport with the color red somewhere on it was bound for a camp like this.

"I think," said Bristol, "that's exactly what makes it insignificant. At most, it means that Metrics has figured out what color we mark things with. But no one in the Red Sea uses transports actually painted red; it would be too conspicuous. They usually go with little flags or ribbons tied to the grilles, something that can be easily removed."

"Red bulbs in the headlights."

"Mm-hmm. So now we just switch to some other color, some other signal."

"Did you tell the leaders that?"

Bristol groaned and took a swig of hot chocolate. "I did."

"Let me guess. You reported, they threw open the door, tossed you out, slammed the door, then opened it again and pelted this thermos at your head."

"Basically." Bristol leaned over his knees and looked out to the thick woods on the other side of the baseball field. "I get that they don't trust anyone else to be involved—we're all so paranoid in here after what we've all been through—but at a certain point, it seems like we all might kill each other out of loneliness. It's not natural."

Denver sucked on her chapped lips a moment, then cupped her hands together and warmed them with her breath. "Got any more in there?"

"Yeah, but I'm saving it."

"For her."

"Yes." Bristol's eyebrows shot toward his hairline. "Denver, what did I *just say*?"

"I don't know what you're talking about."

"You do. Samara has done nothing but help you. What's your deal with her?"

"I just don't like her. Just a feeling." Denver loved saying that. No one would question any opinion, no matter how unpopular, if the reason for it was "just a feeling." People loved to believe in the power of feelings, even the data-obsessed people of Metrics. It was something she'd picked up from reality TV shows when she was small, and the phrase had worked wonders ever since.

"Hmm."

Denver could tell he wasn't buying it, but the thought of another conversation about Samara exhausted her. Maybe Bristol was right: all this distrust was toxic. And, come to think of it, she'd also been wrong about Stephen when they were first married. Before he'd told her about his work with the Red Sea, she'd seen him as a loser, wasting every evening on video games. It hadn't been until later, when he'd told her that he'd disguised his work to make it appear as if he were playing games, that she'd seen him for what he had been. But that had been different. She was wiser now.

"Look," said Bristol, gesturing toward the sky.

Snow. Just barely there, one whispy-white fleck that might have been an optical illusion until a second one appeared in Denver's peripheral vision.

A woman's head appeared around the corner, already looking cross at Denver and Bristol. Karale, one of the leaders here, apparently had patrol duties that evening. "Come on, break it up," she said. "You know you're not allowed over here." Denver also knew Karale's reaction would have been way more severe if her husband, Stephen, were here with her instead of Bristol. She wasn't totally sure if Karale knew they were brother and sister, but anyone could guess—both siblings had their mother's features: the same wide eyebrows, the same thick eyelashes, the same ebony eyes.

Denver stood up so much faster than Bristol that she finally took his elbow to help him. He handed the thermos to her. A jolt of joy leapt inside her before he said, "Take this to Samara?"

She snatched it, wrapping both hands around the stainless steel. "Sure."

"Thank you."

"See you tomorrow."

Of course, she could drain it before she got back. It wouldn't take long to get out of Bristol's sight, and even if he did see her, she didn't particularly care. He knew her feelings toward Little Miss Screw-Up. He probably didn't expect the luxury to make it all the way to her side of the dorm anyway. And Screw-Up herself would never know.

Denver's hand had to leave the warmth of the thermos for only a second to open the door to the girls' dormitory. Then she walked to Samara's bed and deposited it at her feet. Samara looked up from her book. It seemed easy for her to do—that book was probably boring as hell. "That's from Bristol," Denver said, and immediately turned and walked away. This mayhem that was her new life had changed her in a lot of ways, but there were still a few things she refused to let it touch.

CHAPTER TWO

JUDE REEDER COULDN'T BELIEVE HIS LUCK. LAST NIGHT, MISS Shepherd had come in with a new book for him, and today, they were snowed in—none of them were even allowed to go to breakfast this morning—and the way the leaders were talking, maybe not even lunch. It was no big deal for him, since he had snacks in his backpack if he needed them. He would just have to find a way of eating those without anyone else noticing. He told himself he wasn't really hungry yet anyway, so he didn't have to work that out just yet.

He preferred reading all day to eating in the crowded mess hall, but he especially preferred it to working. Just like prison, there were no days off, no time to rest and do exactly what you wanted. All day, he helped do laundry for the compound, including gathering water from the nearby lake and scrubbing sheets and shirts and other men's underwear before hanging it to dry in the meeting hall. It was a little more difficult with only one hand, but he tried his best to keep pace with the rest of the laundry crew. Besides, the extra challenge helped keep his mind from growing too uncharitable—but people were such pigs. How hard was it to keep sauce off your shirt when you ate? There had been no deodorant among them for a long time—why was other people's sweat so much more nauseating than his own? Why were women, just women, so clumsy? He was seriously alarmed when he saw the first streak of blood on a pair of panties and called out to his supervisor that someone had been hurt. The supervisor, a thin woman who had once been heavy, put a kind hand on his shoulder and told him how often women fall down and hurt themselves. She told him it didn't hurt that bad because they were all so used to it. She had that tone that adults sometimes used when speaking to a young child, which, at twelve, Jude was not, and so he distrusted her answer. But then another streak came in, and another, and Jude had no choice but to believe that the ladies had serious balance issues. He needed a break from panties.

He longed to do what Stephen, Bristol, and Samara did: protect the compound from intruders and infiltrators. But everyone had the same choral retort when he asked to leave laundry behind and join the patrol: he was too young.

His stomach growled and he firmly glued his eyes to the next word on the page until it stopped. Tommy, one of the monastery leaders, stopped in front of Jude's bed and let a barely audible whistle out from his teeth. Jude lowered the book.

"Jade, is it?"

"Jude, sir."

"I'm Tommy."

"I know, sir."

The man sat down on the bunk at Jude's feet and rifled through his satchel. "Got something in here for you...I know we're all going a little stir-crazy in here all day, but this should at least keep those sound effects away." He pulled out a protein bar and handed it to Jude. "We're just going around telling everyone that it's all going to be fine. Eat up, and we'll make an announcement in about an hour."

Jude had never been this close to one of the leaders before.

From this distance, he could smell the cigarette smoke on his beard and hoped it wouldn't seep into his quilt. He nodded. "Yes, sir."

Tommy walked to the next bunk, and the sound of crinkling wrappers being opened was suddenly audible.

Tommy walked over to the next bunk. Now that Jude was no longer in the world of Dickens, he was aware of the crinkles of ten or so wrappers being opened and tossed aside. He opened his own and ate slowly. Jude heard Bristol's voice in his head, something he'd said when they'd first arrived and the leaders had put him in a separate dormitory from the others: *We don't have to like it here. We just have to survive until the next phase.*

Just survive. So what if the leaders wouldn't let them out for dinner either? And what about tomorrow? How would he survive? *Just wait until their announcement, then figure something out.* He firmly raised his book back to his face, but after the same sentence passed before his eyes three, four, five times with no meaning, he put it down and turned his head to observe the others. Almost everyone was on some version or another of an ancient electronic device. Things way before Data Watches, like VideoBoys and GamePads. They were all offline, of course, but Jude still didn't know why anyone would use them. He'd tried a GamePad before, and it made him sluggish and dream about things like catching trolls in a gem cave or shooting lasers at monsters. He liked his dreams better when he was reading and talking to people he liked.

Scanning the room, his eyes caught those of another boy for a second too long, and he looked away with burning cheeks. *pleasedon'ttalktome, pleasedon'ttalktome, don'tdon'tdon'tnononono.* Jude snapped his book back up to his face, and after several long moments, glared over the top at the boy again. He was back to his game. Heavier-set and pouty-faced, he stared into his screen with the earliest shadow of a wrinkle between his eyebrows. He must have just wanted to stretch his eyes.

"Boys?"

Jude flinched, but no more than usual. They'd used that same address at the Fox County Detention Center.

"Boys, can everyone hear me?" Tommy stood near the door with his fingers interlaced and his palms flat against his chest, undeniably uncomfortable to be speaking to all thirty of them at once. After a few seconds passed without anyone giving any indication whether or not they could, in fact, hear him, he went on. "So there's still snow on the ground, and our sources on the outside say we'll get more as the day goes on. So we've decided to make the switch, just until spring, to switch day and night. Okay?"

Jude could tell he wasn't the only one who didn't understand. The boys turned their heads toward each other with narrowed eyes amid mumbles.

"Okay, what that means is"—Tommy stopped to giggle—"and I can see where that's confusing, um—we're going to turn days and nights around. From now on, we'll sleep during the day. When the sun sets, we'll get up and get on with our work. We'll eat our meals at night. We'll socialize at night. And if we need to have any meetings, we'll do those at night, too. Before daybreak, a few of us will brush away footprints so they aren't seen if any drones fly over. So we'll start right now. So it's noon now, we'll get ready for bed, then in fifteen minutes, it'll be lights out. I'll wake you back up at eight."

Jude slept horribly. Hours later, when he finally did manage to drift off, he dreamed that he caught the eyes again of the boy in the opposite bed, but this time, the boy was Kopecky. His only friend from the prison—indeed, the only friend in his life—Koepcky had been murdered by Metrics months ago, and Jude had witnessed his death. Jude was surprised to see him, then, in the bunk holding a GamePad, but he could not look away. Kopecky's face was sunken enough to see the clear outline of his skull under his gray flesh. He opened his mouth and raised his hand, and Jude, knowing this was a dream but an important one, leaned in to hear what message he'd come to deliver. Out of his mouth came the agitated voice of Tommy.

Boys, calm down, calm down!

Kopecky disappeared and Jude opened his eyes to the underside of the pillow he'd lodged over his head. He could still see daylight—it couldn't be eight o'clock yet.

"Mister, those guys are out and they're goin' to the mess hall!" one of the boys was saying to Tommy.

"I see that, thanks. I don't know why...could mess up the whole plan..." Tommy dragged on his boots and swung his arms into a coat. "Stay here. I'll find out what's going on."

Jude stood to look out the front window. Indeed, though the sun was just setting, there was a trickle of men going in the direction of the mess hall, though no lights appeared to be on there.

A boy next to Jude snorted. "Plan."

Though Jude wasn't wearing his glasses, he recognized him as the boy who'd turned into Kopecky in his dream. The boy crossed his arms and turned his head toward Jude. "The only plan they got is to hold us here until we all die."

"Hacks! Dumbasses!" shouted another boy.

"We're going to die in here?" the smallest boy, about four, barely got the last word of his question out before he began openly weeping.

"See what you did?" his older brother said to the boy beside Jude.

"He might as well know. We might as well accept it!"

"If we were good at accepting defeat, we wouldn't be here! If you're going to preach that shit, then you don't belong with us!" The older brother punched the heavy boy in the face with a sound that made Jude positive his nose was broken. The boy tried to fight back, but there were arms around both of them now, pulling both boys in opposite corners of the room. Amid the voices shouting and the arms swinging and the feet stamping, Jude stayed in the middle of the room, rooted to the spot where the fight had started, dismayed. He could see Tommy outside, ignored by the men passing him, still in search of someone he could question.

CHAPTER THREE

LIFE HAD TAKEN ON SOME VERY DIFFERENT COLORS FOR BRISTOL. Looking out over the tree stand where he kept watch over the monastery, he saw nothing but a mess of brown shades where the brush latticed over the gray sky. At least the snow had been pretty when it was here. All that remained of it now were translucent clumps. The mud and the dead grass were visible underneath.

Bristol hadn't drawn or painted in months. Images still came to him, once in a while, but not with the vividness and vigor they once appeared. It was like they sensed something was up, that he had neither the time nor the materials to bring them into fruition, and went off in search of another artist. Probably one living far away, in a country where people were free to do things like make art for pleasure.

Probably one who'd do it better than me anyway.

Bristol shook that thought away. Why did those kinds of thoughts plague him here? It wasn't like he'd never experienced inadequate feelings about his abilities before, when he was on the outside of this place, but it was different here. He'd never been really free when living in his mother's apartment, of course, but it was just the air he breathed; he was used to that kind of confinement. This kind was different: the people looking after him to make sure he didn't step out of line were real *people,* not robots or cameras or systems. They had faces that showed disappointment, like when he dipped into the office's dwindling supply of pencils to draw on the smooth underside of a piece of bark. For three months, he sought out the right trees, stripped them, wore out the pencil, and sharpened it with his knife. When his supervisor found what he'd been doing, he pointed out that Bristol had endangered the lives of hundreds of people. What if someone found all those stripped trees? There was nothing in this forest to cause that kind of damage. What if someone found his work? Anyone from the city would immediately know who he was and approximately where he was hiding. It wouldn't take Metrics long to find all of them. Ashamed and, for the first time, afraid, Bristol had stopped.

There was another reason Bristol hadn't created anything in three months. Samara was also part of the watch. Her tree stand was only about fifty yards away from Bristol's. Although he was serious about keeping the monastery safe, it was undeniably boring to let all those shades of brown take over his vision and make it fuzzy. He looked at her tree whenever he could.

Bristol heard a bobwhite calling behind him. He'd only seen a real one once, so he quickly turned his stiff neck around to see if it was a live bird. It was not. The next watchman was here, walking almost silently to Bristol's tree. Bristol smiled, nodded at him, and began to climb down.

"They need y'all at the meetin' house," the young man said.

Bristol wasn't sure he'd heard him correctly. He blinked and leaned in. "Is there a meeting?"

"We just had it. They're wanting to tell y'all next."

"Thanks. Good luck tonight."

The young man nodded and moved past Bristol, climbing up the same way he'd come down.

Bristol stood at the tree a moment, waiting for Samara's relief watchman to arrive, but no one came. She caught his eye and waved him on, possibly smiling, but it was hard to tell under that scarf she wore over the bottom half of her face.

He walked toward the main cluster of buildings, marveling how his body could be in such pain at such a young age. His hips creaked; his knees ached. He tried not to think of that while he walked through the forest as he'd been taught: mindfully, gazing at each place his foot would hit so his journey would be silent. It was a two-mile walk to the meeting house, and this style of walking was excruciatingly slow, but whenever he wanted to speed it up, he visualized the faces of the ones he was protecting. Samara. Denver. Jude. Stephen.

After about fifteen minutes, he heard a rustling behind him and turned. Samara was walking forward at a much faster pace; the world's fastest tortoise. Bristol frowned and waited with his feet planted.

"Slow down," he whispered when she was close enough to hear.

Samara pulled the scarf down from her mouth. "I wanted to catch up with you."

"I can see that. But I heard you."

"Yes, yes." Samara's eyes rolled playfully.

"Here's the part where you say I'm grumpy."

"You *are*. I'm being careful. I just don't think you're used to sitting so much. You have to do what you can to keep yourself active. You're too used to standing and working. You never had to sit in a classroom for every waking hour in a day."

"True," Bristol said and sucked the part of his lip that had broken in the cold.

Samara made a little tutting noise and squeezed his hand to make him stop. She pecked him on the cheek and made him smile. Her eyes found his lips. "Is that painful?"

"What?"

"You need some Vaseline. There's some in our dorm. I'll bring it to you if you want to stop there first."

"They need us at the meeting house."

"I heard that, too. After the meeting, then. I wonder what it's about?"

They wondered the rest of the way, until they were on the blessed dirt road that led them past the buildings: first, the field on the right; then, the girls' and boys' dorms on either side; then, the dining hall beside the girls' dorm. The meeting hall was at the end of the road, and the doors opened straight out into it. Bristol held the door for Samara and relished the little sigh of pleasure she made.

Besides the mess hall, it was the only building with a fireplace that was only sometimes lit. It wasn't just now, but they could tell it had been. The warmth from that fire and from the many living, breathing, heat-creating bodies that had obviously been in and out of the room was still present, and Bristol took his hands out of his pockets to soak it up.

The three leaders of the monastery—Tommy, Karale, and Danovan—sat on folding chairs at the front. Tommy stood when he saw them. "Come in! Come in!"

They were already in, but they walked closer to the front. Tommy sat down again, but there were no more chairs near, so Bristol and Samara took a chair each and brought it with them to the front.

They got all the way to the front of the room when Karale eyed their chairs and said, "You won't need those. This can be short."

Bristol turned to put his back, but Samara unfolded her chair and sat on it. "I'll sit anyway. We've had a long walk here," she said.

Bristol smiled and unfolded his, too. Karale chuckled and glanced from Tommy to Danovan. "I forgot. Well if you'd rather sit for just a few minutes, by all means..."

The five of them were there for no less than an hour. In the first ten minutes, while the three in front argued about an exact date to begin the day-to-night switch, Bristol looked over at Samara's face and saw the fine lines in her young forehead deepen with concern. Samara held up both hands and said, "Tommy, you are saying exactly what Karale and Danovan are saying. The night of the sixteenth *is* the morning of the seventeenth, if the switch happens after midnight."

"Thank you," breathed Danovan, and the three of them began arguing over precisely what hour after midnight.

Bristol's lower back ached. *Just tell us,* he begged in his head. *Just tell us what to do and we'll do it.* He was aware that this thinking was in line with Metrics—the very system they were trying to free themselves from—but he was tired and hungry for more affection from Samara, who was obviously agitated from this meeting. The voices in the room didn't make sense anymore. He let his eyes close for a second.

Suddenly the room was silent. Bristol opened his eyes and saw Samara standing at her full height, arms at her side, staring at Danovan.

"Thank you," she said to break the silence. "Listen to me. The switchover will happen on midnight on the night of the sixteenth and the morning of the seventeenth. You do not have to worry about anyone understanding that. They will understand. Sound good?"

They nodded.

"Thank you." She looked at Bristol, who took that as his cue. He stood and folded his chair as she said, "I assume this means our shifts won't change, since Bristol and I work nights. Thanks for letting us know, though."

"Sure!" said Tommy. "Take care!"

"No, wait!" Karale interjected. "We wanted to let you know that we have a new role for you, Samara. And Bristol, you too."

Danovan rolled his shoulders back and reached his hands back to give himself a little massage. "You'd better sit back down."

They did. Karale said, "Samara, we've been thinking of the children in the group. We know you have experience with education, and we feel that it's essential that the children be confident in some basic skills before we make the move to Canada.

Starting tomorrow at nine, you'll teach for a few hours every day in this room. Just in the mornings. And then you'll follow the kids while they do their work to do some one-on-one sessions with the ones who need extra help."

Bristol's lower back no longer bothered him. He sat stiff in his seat. Samara asked, "What kind of skills?"

"Reading. Writing. Basic math."

"Who will be with Bristol?"

"We discussed it this morning." For the first time since he walked into the room, Karale's eyes found Bristol's. "Your friend Jude will join you. He's excused from laundry. We're cutting down on that, since the clothes take longer to dry now anyway."

It took you one morning to decide that? Heat swelled in Bristol's belly. He looked at Samara, who, on the surface at least, seemed perfectly composed.

"Fine. Nine a.m.? That's only a few hours away. I'd better get to sleep. Has Jude been told?"

They shook their heads. Samara sighed. "Bristol can tell him. He'll need to get to bed sometime today too, to get ready for the night. Now may we go?"

After another friendly, parting "Take care!" from Tommy, Bristol and Samara walked out. When the large sheet metal doors were safely closed behind them, he enclosed Samara in his arms. Through his coat, he could feel her broken breath. She said something, but his coat muffled it.

"What?" he asked.

"They're hopeless," she said. "Completely hopeless. We're never going to get to Canada."

"We can't think like that."

"Why do they want me to teach the kids? They must not think they're going to school anytime soon. They're going to wait all winter to move us. If we move at all."

"Stop it. I mean it. They've got a point. If any of the kids get separated for any reason, they'll need to know how to read maps and count money and stuff, right? And it probably won't be for too long." He could tell she wanted to protest again, but he wasn't going to let her. "We're leaving, Samara. It's just a matter of when. Have a little faith."

His voice, to his own ears, sounded so confident that he almost convinced himself.

CHAPTER FOUR

JOJO WASN'T QUITE GETTING IT, BUT SOMETHING TOLD SAMARA he was close. She took some acorns out of her pocket. "Count as I put these on the table," she said to Joseph. He twisted in his seat so that the top and bottom halves of his body reached away from each other on opposite sides of the chair. Samara knew she still had him by the way his eyes followed the acorns.

JoJo counted to twelve.

"Twelve acorns. Now you have three friends, and you want to divide these evenly between your friends."

JoJo's head dropped below the table. "I can't divide!"

"Fine. No dividing. Just give this acorn to one friend. Here." She pointed to one spot. He took the acorn and thunked it down. She smiled. "Now give this one to another friend. Now to friend number three. Now to friend number four."

He gave her a broad-mouth smile and clasped his hands on the desk, the way schools on the outside require. "I did it!"

"But you still have some left over!"

His face fell. "Oh..."

"It's okay. We'll just give some more out. First to friend number one...then another to friend number two..."

They went through this three more times before he could answer the question on the page. *12* divided by *4* = *?* Karale had taken the liberty of making some notes, and Samara was determined that JoJo and the other kids would learn all—not just some—of Karale's recommended skills within a few weeks.

"One more time. What is twelve divided by four?"

"Three." He said it with a confident tone and a straight back, but he leaned slightly away, toward the door.

Samara smiled. "You can go now."

He leapt away and was out the door before she could stand up. She gathered the acorns in her hand and opened the window to throw them out.

"Hey!"

A man had walked in front of the window. The acorns had bounced across the top of his head on their way to the ground.

"I'm so sorry!" said Samara. "I didn't realize you were there."

The man looked at her and smiled. She knew that smile. It happened sometimes on the outside, but more often, without their injections that kept their minds off such things, she saw it here. She looked at the acorns on the ground.

"You didn't know. I've been trying to do what they tell us to do —you know, walk close to buildings."

Samara had not heard this announcement, but she thought it was probably just another thing she'd missed working the night watch with Bristol. "I'll be sure to look next time."

He got very close to the window. "What's your name?"

"Samara."

"I'm Taye."

They shook hands. Samara realized it was the first physical contact she'd had with someone besides Bristol in six months. "Well," she said, "don't let me stop you."

"I'm coming in there. With you."

Startled, Samara gaped at him. "What?"

"We're co-workers, you and me. I was an education manager before this too. We've got two more kids coming at noon. One for you; one for me. I think one needs reading and the other needs writing."

Samara went back to the table and checked her notes from Karale. Sure enough, there were two kids slotted for appointments with her. She just thought she'd work with them both. Taye came in the front door and plopped his own notebook on the table next to hers.

"So when'd you get here, Samara?"

"Back in July."

"I came in August. Man, what a weird life to get used to, huh? After how we used to live?"

Samara nodded, aware that he thought she was a Three. It made sense; it was highly unusual for her, as a Five, to have gotten a job as an education manager. But even that, the job assignment officers had decided, had been too good for her. Not a mistake. They'd never admit to making a mistake. But they did correct their little surprise as soon as they could by making her the tutor to an entire juvenile prison population. That had been where she had met and ultimately freed Jude. They would never have let her in a real school, where she'd have taught alongside Threes, like Taye. Something about this made her angry, that he was still carrying around this false and unfair ranking system that had governed their lives before St. Mary's. She didn't feel like engaging. As much as she'd wished for more friends before this moment, she wished he'd act as cold and uninterested as the rest of the people here. She said nothing and took out the book she'd planned to use for the student coming in a few minutes.

"Which one would you like to take, the reader or the writer?"

"Oh, you can have the writer," he said, showing his brilliant teeth. Samara wondered if he'd bothered to notice hers yet. They weren't terrible, but one look at her mouth would tell him that she was no Three.

The door opened again and two people walked inside: a little girl, about ten years old, and...

"Tommy?" asked Samara with a raised eyebrow. "Is something wrong?"

"Hello, Samara. Taye." Tommy nodded at them and twisted the ends of his scarf in his hands. "No, nothing's wrong...well, something... see, Karale and Danovan want me to get some help with my writing."

Taye flashed his bright teeth at the little girl and beckoned her to the open book on the table. Samara worked with Tommy for a long hour in which she discovered that he wasn't a terrible writer, apart from the misspellings and the slippery grip on grammar and the tendency to use exclamation points in place of almost any other form of punctuation. When she suggested they try another exercise, he groaned.

"I don't understand why I have to sit here like a schoolboy. Karale and Danovan do most of the writing, anyway," he said.

Samara kept her face toward the table. "What kinds of things do they write?"

"Letters. To this congressman at Metrics. I don't remember his name. They're always calling him the Bird, though. He wants to help us but we're trying to figure out just how."

Taye looked up sharply. Tommy flinched. "I mean," Tommy said, "I shouldn't have said that. Don't tell anyone I said that."

"We won't." Samara put her hand on Tommy's. "Your writing is really pretty good; it only needs some tweaks here and there. In a few weeks, you'll be writing those letters yourself."

Tommy went back his exercises with a light blush on his forehead. Samara and Taye glanced at each other darkly while the little reader continued to butcher Harry Potter.

After their students left, Samara and Taye folded the table and carried it off the side wall together.

"Did you know that?" asked Taye.

"That someone from Metrics knows we're here?" asked Samara. "Not exactly. I did wonder how we were getting our supplies. I figured we were getting help from other chapters."

"Of what?"

"Of the Red Sea. I don't know much about the scope, but there have to be others around."

Taye shook his head. "There are no other chapters. No one else. We're it. I'm almost positive that no one else survived the relocation."

Samara thought of those she knew who were not here. Nan. Lydia. The two women who had saved her when she was stuck in a tree with a dislocated shoulder, who had sheltered and fed her and Bristol and Jude when they knew the risks they faced. She lowered her head and closed her eyes.

Taye clasped his hands on both her shoulders. "We've all lost someone."

Samara stepped away and folded her chair. "It's a problem that the leaders have been communicating with Metrics without telling us. We need to talk with them about it."

Taye snorted. "What we need are new leaders."

"Here?"

"Here and there. Inside and out. Camp and country."

"I think Karele and Danovan are doing it this way just because it's what we're used to—following the directions of a closed group. We need to think of something else. Something more open to everyone."

Taye nodded. "Sounds messy."

"Maybe."

"Are you going to talk to them about it?"

"I don't see why not. Are you going to join me?"

He stepped in front of her as if he were going to take her chair, but instead of taking it, he stayed standing with his hands on it. "Of course I will."

"Excuse me."

Samara dropped the chair. Denver stood in the doorway in a pink-and-yellow-striped apron over her coat.

"Denver!" said Samara. "I didn't see you come in."

"I noticed. We saved some food for you. It's ready now." Denver turned and left in one swift motion.

Taye ambled over to collect his own book bag. "You coming?"

"You can have mine. I'm going back to bed."

Samara was so tired that the skin around her eyes hurt, but she had so much more to do, much more to think about. Life was much more complicated than it had been an hour ago. She walked out the door, where her feet immediately hit the dirt road.

CHAPTER FIVE

DENVER STOOD FIRM ON HER FEET AND TWISTED HER TORSO from side to side. A warm front had moved in, but she was perpetually cold. She peeped over the side of the building, watching the field. Finally, a figure broke off from the road and walked in her direction. She kept watching it until she could see him grin at her.

"Finally." Stephen took Denver's face in his hands, and she breathed in the solace of his kiss.

"I've missed you," said Denver.

"I've missed you, too." Stephen placed his hands on her hips and pulled her in tighter. Denver took a step back but kept her arms around him.

"Not tonight."

"What's wrong?"

"I think I'm sick."

"Sick?" Stephen frowned and put a hand on her forehead. "You don't feel warm."

"It feels like a stomach bug, but it comes and goes." She didn't mention her other symptoms, mostly because they were hard to define—her skin was too sensitive now, to touch and to cold. She wanted to shed it, to cringe away from it and free herself from constant shivers. And she was extremely tired now, after doing mundane things like carrying a five-pound bag of flour across the kitchen floor, or walking five minutes to her dorm or the field. She was ashamed to admit it, but what she wanted more than anything these days was a good nap.

"Have you been to the infirmary yet?"

"No. I forgot we had one."

"Let's go now. They might have something there to help. It might make it easier to sleep if your stomach's been bothering you."

Denver smiled and slid her arm through his. They walked on the road, kicking pebbles now and then, until they got to the end of row of dorms.

"I think it's in this one." Stephen pointed to one of the boys' cabins.

"In there?"

"No, there's an attachment to the back of it. We'll go around."

The infirmary, tucked away behind the bustling dorm, was a pleasant little place. From the look of it, someone had taken considerable care to organize and tidy it. There was a row of shelves stocked scantily with bottles of liquid and tablets along the back wall, and two little twin beds on either side of those shelves, both made up with cheery yellow quilts and fluffy pillows. The corners of Denver's mouth impulsively shot up. It was always good to see someone care.

A door in the corner opened and a woman walked out, drying her hands on a tea towel. Denver recognized her tight gray curls from the mess hall line. She'd never bothered to wonder what her work assignment was. The little lady peered at them though half-moon glasses on a chain.

"May I help you?"

Stephen stepped forward and stretched out his hand. "Yes, I'm

Stephen, and this is my wife, Denver. We think she has a stomach bug."

"But it comes and goes," said Denver.

"Please sit down," the nurse gestured to one of the beds. "I'm Nurse Sue. I may have something for you, but I need to deliver some medicine to another dorm first. My little diabetes patient in Dorm Three. Can I ask you to wait here?"

"My pleasure," said Denver. As soon as it came out, she knew it was a weird thing to say—and still it was the truth. No room had felt more like home since she arrived here.

Nurse Sue smiled. "Be right back. Lie down if you need to."

She walked out, and Denver lay back on the pillow, which sank under the weight of her head. She moaned. Stephen sat next to her.

"What's wrong?"

"Nothing. It just feels so comfortable. I could stay here forever."

"You seem exhausted."

"I am. And I've had a really strange day..." She turned her head back to him, but kept it on the pillow. "I'm sorry. I haven't even asked how your day went."

He stroked her temple. "It was fine. Why was your day strange?"

"I walked in on something I probably shouldn't have seen."

"What?"

"Samara."

"What was she doing?"

"She was...just getting a little too close to another man. I didn't recognize him. But they were definitely touching, and they seemed embarrassed that I saw." Her eyes suddenly felt heavy. She shut them. "It was kind of exactly what I was hoping for—this kind of thing, something that would make Bristol break it off with her. But now I feel like I can't be the one to tell Bristol. He knows I don't trust her and it'll just sound like I'm making it up. Even if he does believe me, I don't want him to be hurt."

"That makes sense. Are you even sure about what you saw? Were they doing anything...incriminating?"

She yawned. "I can't be sure."

"I'd just leave it for now. He's crazy about her. If she's going to break his heart, she should be the one to do it."

"I don't want to see her play my brother for a fool."

"I don't want to see her play my brother-in-law for a fool."

Denver smiled and opened her eyes. Stephen touched his nose to hers. "Let's leave it for now," he said. "Unless..."

"What?"

"Unless you want to talk to her. Confront her about what you saw and what you're afraid of."

Denver thought for a moment. Ordinarily, that was exactly what she would do. But the plain truth of the matter was that she didn't have the strength. She could barely keep her eyes open. Maybe after some medicine and a few days of rest...

"Then again," Stephen said, "is it possible you misunderstood?"

"No." Denver's answer came out as a defiant impulse.

"No, you never misunderstand anyone."

Denver opened her eyes to find him grinning at her. She frowned deeper to mirror his face inversely. "That was different," she said. "You were a literal secret agent. How was I supposed to know?"

When they'd first married, Denver had thought Stephen was nothing but a common consumer, playing games on his watch all day and expecting her to feed and clean up after him. When Bristol had gone missing, Stephen had revealed to her that he was a volunteer with the Red Sea, the organization that helped the Unregistered across the border so they could live free. When Metrics had discovered him, the two of them had escaped together, camping in the woods with almost no supplies and no way of finding Bristol. Somehow, they'd found him anyway, along with Samara and Jude. Though she'd never admit it, despite the danger, and the cold, and the uncertainty, the months they'd been here in the cold valley had been among the happiest in her life so far. Stephen was here. And whatever she said, even if she didn't mean it, Stephen understood her.

Nurse Sue walked back in, this time fixing the lid back onto a small box. "All done! Now. Oh." She seemed surprised to see the two of them lying so close to each other on the bed. Stephen scrambled onto his feet.

The nurse stuck a thermometer in Denver's mouth and placed a stethoscope on her chest. "No apologies, my dears; I've seen much worse. Now, deep breaths."

She moved the stereoscope around, then took the thermometer out of her mouth and glanced at it. "Hmm," she said. "These stomach troubles...do they feel like sharp pains, or nausea?"

"Nausea."

"When do you feel nauseous?"

"Usually at work. I work in the kitchen here."

"Smelly work?"

"Oh, yes," said Denver, crinkling her nose. "The garlic smells terrible. And the garbage is getting worse. And even some things that don't stink on the outside, they do here."

"Like what?"

"Dried rice. Beans."

The nurse smiled. "People?"

"Yes! Most of all. How did you know?"

The nurse cocked her head and narrowed her eyes. "Tell me something, Denver. I have something in my bag, there on the shelf. What is it?"

Denver looked at the shelf and saw the bag hanging from it. There was no way to tell what was inside by looking at it, but as soon as her nose turned into that direction, she involuntarily sniffed the air. "It's an orange," she said.

Nurse Sue chuckled, reached into the bag, and handed her the orange. "Would you like it?"

"Yes!" Denver said, and then, aware of her eagerness, looked toward the ground. "Yes, please, if you can spare it."

Stephen crossed his arms. "How did you know—"

"Your wife's not sick, Stephen." Nurse Sue crossed the room, took the orange out of the bag, and tossed it to Denver, who caught it one-handed. "She's going to have a baby."

CHAPTER SIX

BRISTOL SULKED ABOUT HAVING LOST HIS GIRLFRIEND'S COMPANY up until he picked Jude up for their walk into the woods. Bristol arrived at the youth cabin just as most of the boys were getting ready for bed—the sound of toilets flushing for the only time of the day could be heard, and most of the boys were taking off their shoes and crawling into their bunks. When Jude saw Bristol at the door, he waved with wild abandon and darted toward him. In the short time Bristol had known Jude, he'd never seen him excited about anything. Come to think of it, it was rare to see someone his age excited at all—God knew he wasn't.

Twelve years old. Denver was only thirteen. That was the beginning and the ending of something between them—both the bridge and the rift. That was the year Metrics stopped educating the Unregistered, and Denver began stage two of schooling. He just needed some time to get used to the idea. Back then, the boredom of unloading produce trucks and peeling carrots at the restaurant was like a physical illness. He felt that boredom in his bones, in his blood, and he wasn't able to wrap his mind around the fact that the rest of his days would be spent this way. This was before he even knew about Drift, the magical powder that took all feeling away and made you empty. He hadn't found it yet, but he longed for its effects daily.

Maybe Denver had known about it and was trying to distract him—maybe that was why she brought home that paper and pencil from her first day of classes. *They're from my architecture class,* she'd said. *I asked the manager if I could have an extra set. Do you still like to draw?* Bristol was wary of this apparent charity, but he took the paper anyway and filled every inch with gloomy images before adding the sheets to the mess under his bed.

Jude brought him back to reality with a hug. Bristol patted his back—a little too firmly—three times, and then ruffled his hair. "Got a hat?"

"No. I had one, but it was stolen."

"Stephen's got one. He's part of the day watch, so when he gets to the stands, we'll ask to borrow his. You'll need it for the night."

The two of them set forth in the forest, and Bristol noticed that Jude was a fast learner. He was walking almost as quietly as Bristol by the time they reached their destination. Stephen was happy to lend his hat, practically giddy in fact. Bristol watched Jude attempt to climb the tree three times before deciding he needed a boost. He made a basket with his interlaced fingers and vaulted him up onto a branch. When they were both high in their own trees, Bristol said, "You're going to have to practice that."

"I'll get it eventually."

"If we see anything, we'll need to get down fast. You need to work on your strength and your hip mobility if you're going to do this job right."

Jude nodded and looked down at the ground. "It's harder with one hand."

Bristol sighed. It was easy to forget that; Jude never complained. "I'm sorry. I just..."

"...miss Samara."

"Yes."

Bristol chortled. He'd done it again—he'd underestimated the intelligence of this kid. How many times would he have to learn the same lessons?

"She's doing a great job, though," chimed Jude. "There's this boy in my cabin—JoJo—And she taught him how to divide. On the *first day*."

Not surprising, Bristol thought, and beamed from his tree. "Thanks for letting me know that. She's a teacher. That's just who she is. You're right—it was a waste to keep her perched up here. We should stop talking now, Jude."

"We don't talk?" It was getting dark, so Bristol couldn't see the look on Jude's face, but he could tell it he was disappointed. "Then what do we do?"

"Watch. Listen. Think."

"I'm hungry."

"Doesn't your tree have a popcorn maker?"

"That's not funny."

"Look, I'd give you food if I had any. Just focus on watching."

"And listening. And thinking."

"That's right."

The night passed slowly for Bristol. His mind was heavy with the same worries: the monastery was mismanaged. With every interaction he had with the leaders, he could see the cracks more and more clearly. They were incoherent. They were uneducated—like himself—but painfully unaware of it, and not interested in growing—quite unlike himself. They were petty. They didn't listen. They didn't trust anyone.

For having lived in it all of his life, Bristol had no idea how the Metric Government worked. Perhaps that was by design. But he could see similarities. A small percentage of people making all the decisions, assigning jobs, deciding what was best for the larger population. And the larger population just went along with it all, following the leader. *Simon says jump.*

The major difference between Metrics' leaders and these ones was that Metrics seemed to be smart. Although they made sweeping decisions without any rationale, no one in the world even knew their names or what they looked like! Even if they did want to question those decisions, no one would know who to turn to. There had to be a better way. A new way.

It was times like these, when Bristol was thinking hard and needed inspiration, that new pictures would come flashing into his head. Back when he was painting, when the channel for such inspiration was open, it would come to him without having to ask. But nothing was coming. A dullness seeped into his mind as his sight hardened onto his hands. He closed his eyes. He'd never tried talking to it—this thing that gave him those images. Bristol glanced over at Jude's tree, then back at his hands. "Please," he whispered, too softly for Jude to hear, "Please give me a vision. Tell me how to fix this."

He saw something—not a clear something, but a something nonetheless. Three people in front of a crowded room, like the leaders in front of the big group. Then, next to it, another image: people sitting in chairs in a giant circle. *That's absurd.* Bristol shook his head. He tried asking the thing for another image. Nothing, nothing, nothing. He took some dead leaves in his hand and crushed them. Then he arranged the pieces of the leaves in those images—three pieces in front of many, then many pieces in a circle. He could feel Jude watching him. He brushed the pieces away and put his eyes back on the forest.

When the sun came back up, Bristol asked if Jude was ready, and the two of them climbed down and started back.

"I've been thinking," said Jude.

"Good."

"About the leaders. I don't know what needs to change, but the day-to-night mixup a few days ago gave me an idea."

"What idea?"

"I think something has to change. A different way of doing

things altogether. The day-to-night changeover is set for the night of the sixteenth, right? At midnight?"

"Yeah?"

"Well, what if we told everyone except Tommy, Karale, and Danovan to wake up one hour earlier, so we could all talk about what to do? We can't gather with them around, but we need to have a talk. If we let things stand as they are, they're going to let us down. Then we'll have wasted our time here."

"So wake up an hour earlier..."

"And decide what to do. When they wake up and find us all gone, they'll probably go to the meeting house. Then we can tell them the new plan. If everyone agrees, that's two hundred people against three—they'll step down."

"We'll have one hour to figure this out."

"Basically. Yeah."

It sounded crazy, but so did most good ideas. *How many times do you have to learn the same lessons?*

Jude bit his lip. "You think I'm sleep-deprived?"

"No. I think you're brilliant."

CHAPTER SEVEN

SAMARA EYED THE SKY AND WRAPPED HER ARMS AROUND herself. JoJo was still at his work assignment today, so she had a little break between teaching all the children at once and teaching Tommy. She stood outside, hoping to catch some sunlight, but clouds had moved in, strong and gray as sheets of steel. *Stratus.*

The cold air shocked her lungs, but she breathed deeply anyway and started walking toward the mess hall. It would be busy now, but she could think of no better time to talk to Denver about the plan. The mess hall and the cabins were really the only two places where free conversation could still happen, and conversation from the crowd would create a nice buzz to cover what she had to say.

Even though the food wasn't hot, the inside of the mess hall was still about ten degrees warmer. The warmth of many bodies carrying their trays to the tables and sitting in tight rows was a relief from the constant shivering.

Samara saw Denver assembling sandwiches and potato chips on trays and handing them out. Samara stood in line. Denver, she noticed, looked at her and then turned back to the trays. Samara couldn't tell if she didn't see her or if she was pretending not to.

Samara had been inside enough female friendships to recognize a cold shoulder, but still couldn't quite figure out how or if she deserved it.

When it was Samara's turn to be handed a tray, she said, "I need to talk to you privately. Can you get away?"

Denver's eyes flickered to Samara's, then back down at the chips. "Wait until the line's gone. I'll come to you."

Samara hoped there was no inkling of surprise in her face as she nodded and made her way to a table. She wished she could squeeze between strangers for warmth and make small talk, but she sat at the end of a table instead and waited for Denver. Maybe she had been misreading her all along. Her dad had helped her see things like this more clearly. Whatever her problem, he'd ask how else her situation could be interpreted. With his help, she could see interactions like this from many different angles. Samara hoped that her mom and dad had found each other again after she'd run away—she hoped, with a begging intensity, that at this moment, they were together.

A waving hand in her peripheral made her turn. Taye. How had she forgotten? It was always his lunch hour. She didn't know what else to do except smile. He sat next to her, closer than necessary.

"No JoJo today?" he asked.

"Not today. They needed him on..." Samara stopped. Come to think of it, she didn't have the slightest idea what his employment assignment was. "I don't know. Probably laundry."

"No, the laundry guys are all here." Taye gestured down the table. "Best part of their day. My little brothers are there."

Samara had been looking at Denver, trying to catch her eye, trying to communicate silently that she'd get rid of this guy in just a second—but now she raised her eyebrows at Taye. "Brothers?"

"Yeah. I'm the first, so I got all the good stuff. Always felt bad for them, though. I mean, they're still little so they were in school, but I knew how they were going to have it when they turned twelve. My mom had the idea to take them out before they had the chance to send them away. Lucky thing, too. That was just a day before the relocation." He pointed. "That's Cork, and the little one is Henry."

Samara knew better, by now, than to ask where his mother was. She waved at the two boys. Cork reddened and looked back at his friend across the table, but Henry gave her a cobble-toothed grin.

Taye snorted and waved back. "Cute little guy, huh? I never understood why they fix all of our teeth exactly the same. Takes all of the character out of the face, don't you think?"

He looked at her pointedly. She ran the tip of her tongue along the roof of her mouth, along the bump where a permanent tooth still lurked on top of a baby one that had never fallen out. "If you want to know my Tier, just ask."

"Okay, fine. Your teeth are interesting. Why is that?"

"I'm a Five. *Was* a Five."

"You said you were an education manager."

"I was. Metrics assigned me the job, but they couldn't—or wouldn't—move my Tier. So I worked in a juvenile detention center. That's where I met Jude."

"Jude Reeder? My brothers work with him. He's a...special kid." The tone he said it in suggested there was more he wanted to say —none of it nice—but was watching Samara for her reaction.

"I know. That's why I helped him escape."

They looked hard at each other, sizing the other up.

Taye broke the gaze first. "Then you've got just as much at stake here as I do. You were just as scared as I was to hear that stuff about the Bird."

Denver approached the table, but did not sit. "Am I interrupting?"

"No, nothing," Samara said. "Denver, this is my coworker, Taye. He was an ed manager on the outside, too. Taye this is my—my friend, Denver."

Denver nodded curtly. "You wanted to talk?"

"Yes, but..." She glanced back at Taye, who shoved three unbroken chips into his mouth at once. "Oh, he might as well know, too. Taye and I heard something slip from Tommy." She told

Denver about how the leaders were communicating with a Metrics official; then, she relayed the whole of Jude's plan to wake the entire camp before midnight to discuss more options.

Denver listened with an expression Samara had never seen before; a mix of doubt and fear. When Samara was finished explaining Jude's plan, Denver asked, "So what do you want from me?"

"I want you and Taye to help get the word around. Go to people you trust and tell them."

Denver gave a chesty laugh. "People we trust? You've been on the watch with Bristol for too long. People don't trust people here."

Taye nodded. "She's right, Samara. Most people have just one person they talk to here, maybe two. But it's not a friendly place."

Samara paused a beat and looked around. Sure enough, though the room was abuzz, there were no bobbing heads jumping from conversation to conversation. Those heads were together in pairs or small groups of three. Now that she saw it, she saw that it fit with her own experience in the dorm. She just thought they weren't talking to her because she was asleep all day and awake all night. They weren't talking to her because they never knew her on the outside.

"Okay," said Samara. "New plan, then. Listen in as much as you can. See if you can hear complaints about the leaders."

"That should be easy," said Taye. "Nobody's happy with them. Nobody's willing to do anything about it, either."

"Because they're scared," said Denver. "Most of us have exactly one experience challenging authority. And it's what landed us in this mess, where we feel like there are no other options."

Taye and Samara looked at Denver. It was most Samara had ever heard her say, and it was also true.

"If they're scared," said Samara, "then they'll be glad we can help them. We have to let them know."

"They don't trust us. They'll turn us in."

"It's a risk we'll have to take. Wait until they're complaining.

Then tell them the plan. We'll hash something out and when the leaders come find us, we'll tell them the new plan. Together."

Denver looked at Samara thoughtfully, with hand curled at her mouth. Then she traced her thumb down to her navel and said, "No. I can't do that. But good luck." She turned and darted back to the kitchen.

I should be used to disappointment by now, thought Samara, but she wasn't quite. Samara wanted to be close to this one person who knew Bristol better than she did, but right now, she would have settled for help in lieu of friendship. It would have meant some sort of relationship, however icy.

"What was that about?" asked Taye.

"What?"

"Didn't you come in with her? Here?"

"Yes."

"Are you fighting?"

"No. I don't think so. We've never been close. But she's my boyfriend's sister. I thought she'd want to help. But it doesn't matter. I know she won't give us away." Samara turned her attention back to Taye. "So, will you do it?"

"On two conditions. One, you think up a few ideas to present to the group so we're not going in blind. One hour is really not enough time to come up with a whole new way of governing ourselves here. We'll need a little push from you."

"That sounds reasonable. What's the other condition?"

"Don't mention your boyfriend again."

CHAPTER EIGHT

Jude was on a slightly different schedule now, but it didn't matter. When he woke up, the rest of the boys were getting ready for bed. Jude saw the boy who'd thrown the punch earlier that week walk into the bathroom with his toothbrush. He grabbed his own and, desperately telling himself to *be cool,* slowly followed him. Remembering his words—*If we were good at accepting defeat, we wouldn't be here!*—Jude thought he might be a good start. Since the snow day debacle, there seemed to be little doubt that defeat was coming if things stayed the way they were.

In Jude's books, the heroes were plucked from their unfortunate situations by some benevolent benefactor and launched into a new, wondrous world. In Jude's experience, the real world was exactly the opposite. He had been plucked from the life he knew, yes, but not to be thrust to a better one. He'd been framed for Bristol's vandalism for reasons that were still unclear to him and put into prison. Then, Samara had chosen him, among all of her other students at Fox County Detention Center, to escape with her. They had ended up here, where the clues pointed toward another forceful exit.

No more. He couldn't allow it to happen again. He didn't care that he was young—he'd put blind trust in adults before and wasn't satisfied with where it had led him. If there was going to be another mistake, the least he could do was take responsibility for it.

He was surprised when Bristol liked his idea to stage a coup, and even more surprised when Samara got on board too. It was one of those jarring realizations about growing up—the beginning of being seen as an intellectual equal to adults. He didn't know that the dissatisfaction with the leaders ran so deep. Now that the night of the uprising loomed, they were all moving onto Stage Two of the plan: spreading the word.

A handful of people knew about the plan, but as the only minor, Jude was responsible for telling others in his dorm. But Tommy was always around, and although Jude had used his presence as an excuse for not talking to anyone for the past few days, he was running out of time.

The second sink was open, so Jude stood in front of it, glancing at the boy and then back at his own reflection. Now that he was here, he realized he hadn't really rehearsed how to start off. Should he say hello? Ask him about his day? Just launch right into the speech that he *did* prepare? Jude wondered how much longer the boy would brush. He wondered if he would rinse the sink when he was done.

The boy spat into the sink, raised his shoulders, and turned to Jude. "What?"

Dismayed, Jude let the toothbrush hang from his mouth. "W-what?"

"You're looking at me funny."

"I-I wasn't trying to. But I want to talk to you."

"I don't want to talk about what happened the other day. I just overreacted, okay? I already said sorry to Mullins."

"No—really? That's nice—but that's not what I wanted to talk about. I have something to tell you."

Tommy walked in, grinned at them, and shut the door to a bathroom stall. The boy looked disgusted.

"Outside," he told Jude.

Their shoes and coats were already on—Jude had the feeling he slept in his shoes too—so they walked straight out and toward the field, without having discussed it. When they got close to the building, Jude introduced himself, feeling he should before he asked a favor.

"I'm Cork," the boy said, without taking Jude's hand.

"Jude." He cleared his throat. "I'm worried about Tommy. And Karale. And Danovan. Not just me—lots of people are worried that they're going to make a serious mistake with our security here, or that maybe they already have."

Cork nodded. He kept his gaze on the ground, but his body still leaned in, so Jude guessed he was still listening.

"I've heard," he continued, "from someone I trust, that the leaders are in contact with someone from Metrics."

Cork's head shot up. "No. They wouldn't do that."

Jude swallowed. "They think they're helping us. But if we don't know who they're talking to, they could be putting us in danger."

"How do you know? Do they tell you that kind of stuff if you're on the watch?"

"No. I shouldn't tell you who I heard it from, in case..."

"...in case I'm a narc?" He pressed his jaw tight to his face. "I've got my little brother to protect here. If you've got any information, I want to know it. And if any change is happening, I want to be a part of it."

Jude drew in a shallow breath. "Okay. Here's your chance."

By the night of the 14th—two days before the meeting—all of the boys in the youth dorm knew about the plan and were solemnly sworn to secrecy. Solemn vows, especially against grownups, always seemed to be sacred in the world of children, which Jude recognized as he straddled the two worlds.

The only thing that worried Jude was the change of

atmosphere. Jude hadn't really noticed it before, but now that they all shared a secret, there was a tone of fraternity in the dorm— they still didn't really talk to each other, but they walked together, held doors for each other, passed each other the occasional cigarette and slapped each other on the back in thanks. Jude told Cork of his concerns, positive Tommy would notice the difference in attitude, but Cork just laughed, slapped him on the back, and offered him a drag.

Jude didn't smoke, but that wasn't the only reason he declined. He appreciated Cork for everything that he had done, but going out of his way to make another friend seemed a terrible insult to Kopecky's memory. Jude had gone through life as a loner, as a weirdo, as someone who didn't know what to say to people when they tried to be friendly, and Kopecky was the only peer he'd ever come across who didn't seem to mind. Now that Cork was showing the same traits as his first friend, Jude *wanted* him to mind. He certainly had more experience being a weirdo than a friend, and he preferred to keep it that way, if for no other reason than to remember how special Kopecky really was.

Nevertheless, Jude had done a smart thing in roping in Cork as an early adopter of the coup. The rest of the team hadn't been so lucky. Bristol and Stephen had spread the word among all the men who seemed trustworthy—which wasn't too many of them—but Samara was having a tougher time with the women. There were more men than women here, but, as Samara told him, they had more trouble trusting each other. Since Denver had refused to help, the only woman telling others about the plan was Samara, which made her seem dangerous. Jude had asked why, and Bristol explained it to him.

He said, "When a man makes a friend, they can do it just by sitting together and doing something. If a man fishes next to another man, they can leave the lake as friends. This can work with two of us, or with half a dozen. But it's different for women. They make friends usually one at a time, have a deeper connection. Then, that woman brings in the other to a larger circle. They can't

—or won't—form too many bonds at once. That's why Samara's having trouble."

It didn't sound too complicated to Jude—after all, he'd just talked to one person. It had just been the *right* person, one who didn't mind telling the others sometime during laundry duty. Denver actually seemed like the right person, too—she worked with most of the other women in the kitchen, and she didn't seem to mind being the center of attention. Why wouldn't she help?

On the morning of the sixteenth, while Bristol and Jude were walking home, Samara came zipping through the forest, quiet but far from silent.

"I could hear—" Bristol started.

Samara wore a jubilant smile. "It's Denver. She says she'll help us if we bring her a peach."

Jude was sure he'd misheard her. Bristol must have as well, because he asked, "A peach?"

"A peach."

"Is that code for something?" Bristol asked.

"No, she just wants a peach. To eat. She just has a craving for one, and she says she'll help if we can get that for her."

Bristol rubbed his eyes. "She's being *so* stupid. I don't know what's gotten into her. It's January. How are we going to find a peach?"

Samara wilted. "I thought...I thought Jude might be able to help us."

"Me?" Jude said a little too loudly. Bristol shushed him.

"Yes, you. JoJo's in your dorm, isn't he?"

"Yes, but what does he have to do with it?"

Samara looked over her shoulder, then back at Jude. "I don't know for sure, but I think his employment assignment puts him in a unique position to help."

CHAPTER NINE

BRISTOL WENT STRAIGHT TO THE DINING HALL TO FIND DENVER. He found her there, doing something he used to do every day: prepping food in a clean, white apron. The only difference was that he used to peel and dice real potatoes. She was opening cans of them and draining the water in the large industrial sink.

"Are you crazy?"

She didn't even look up. "Samara told you about the peach?"

"A peach? You want to hold up the future of this whole place for a peach?"

"Please. I don't really want a peach."

"You don't?"

"Well, I do, actually. But more than that, I want to ask for one."

"What's your problem, Den?"

Denver whipped her head up and glared at him, jaw set. "I just wanted to check on something before I drastically change our lives again."

"Check on what?" Bristol noted the bags under her eyes and the grayish cast on her skin. She looked like shit, but now probably wasn't the time to tell her that.

The other ladies in white aprons had begun to observe the siblings, not by looking but by slowing their work and leaning in ever so slightly. Bristol looked at Denver and neither said anything more: one of the advantages of having a sister so close was having a connection close to telepathy. Bristol helped her with the cans, first draining them, then transferring them to the cold metal serving tray. The breakfast line wouldn't start to form for fifteen or so minutes more, so while the other women went outside to smoke and shiver, they stayed inside.

"Okay," said Bristol. "What is it you want, really?"

"I want to know if we have any support. There's a rumor that JoJo is the liaison. He's how we get food."

"Liaison to whom? Who gives us food?"

"Well" —a sly smile spread across Denver's face— "that's what I want to know. I've been curious about how we get fed here ever since we first arrived, but I've only been getting friendly with our delivery man very recently. He used to be a flirt, you see, on the outside. He's Unregistered and never had any focus injections, so maybe he was even a womanizer."

"You know those injections only take away natural impulses. Just because the man has natural impulses doesn't mean he was a womanizer."

"Well, nevertheless, all it took was a little eyelash-batting to loosen up his lips. Anyway, he told me that he takes JoJo to a place far out in the woods; then, JoJo walks by himself to a little ghost town. He waits thirty minutes, then drives to the ghost town himself, and picks up JoJo and all the food for the week. They're going today, right after breakfast."

"How did JoJo get this job? He can't be more than seven."

"That I don't know. And if Stan knows more, he's not telling. But I want to know more. Specifically, I want to know whether we're dealing with Metrics or—"

"The Red Sea? You think there are more of us out there?"

Denver rubbed her temples. "I know they say we're the only

ones left, but if the Red Sea isn't giving us food, who is? It doesn't make sense for Metrics to be doing it."

"Maybe another group? Maybe just some random guy who wants to help?"

"Some random guy would have to have some fabulous connections to feed two hundred people every week, which means he'd have to be part of Metrics, which, as I said, doesn't make sense. I think it's the Red Sea. I just want to be sure. I want to know we've got support before we shake things up here."

"How will asking for a peach make you sure?"

"Easy. I don't know what their relationship with JoJo is, but he's pretty lovable, right?"

Denver was right—JoJo's big eyes, constant smile, and wiry limbs made him look like a doll. He was the kind of kid who made even those most ardent that they'd never apply for a child to stop to reconsider.

Denver continued, "I just want to know the reaction if he asks for something difficult to get. If they give him a peach, or if they promise him one next week, they've got connections in the south, which would be bad news. It wouldn't be safe to destabilize this place with Metrics watching so closely. On the other hand, if they tell him sorry, they just can't do it—"

"—it still wouldn't be a guarantee."

"I've learned to look for clues, not guarantees. It's the best I can do."

"When are you going to tell JoJo?"

"I've already asked him. He was eager to try to help. I told him it was for the baby. That's the other thing, Bristol—you're going to be an uncle."

The earth shakes beneath Bristol's feet. *Earthquake,* he thinks, but Denver is there, saying she wants to give birth now. Bristol pleads with her to wait just one more day. It'll be safer to wait until the earthquake slows. *But I want my baby now,* she says, and reaches down and pulls out the perfect little purple baby, wriggling against her embrace. She holds him tight, but the ground rocks them both and Denver drops him. The baby is carried away by the waves of vibrations. Denver screams. Bristol tries reaching for him, running for him...

Clued in by the fact that his legs wouldn't move, Bristol opened his eyes and took a sharp inhale. Just a dream. He felt the rumbling of the truck bed underneath him. There was more rust on this ancient pickup than paint, and though Bristol didn't see how it would run, he'd unhooked one of the frayed bungees and slid inside the back anyway. A thin sheet covered the bed, and underneath it, he could smell decaying metal and rotting cotton.

They headed off the campus. He heard distant voices behind him, where, in the cab, JoJo's giggle punctuated every few sentences. Bristol felt thankful that he wasn't prone to motion sickness, because there wasn't much room to move. The latch on the back looked loose enough that he could probably unhook it easily, though he couldn't be sure how much noise it would make. It wouldn't matter if he were caught on the way back; he just wanted to go unnoticed until he could ensure that JoJo would be unharmed.

The truck didn't slow much as it came to a halt. Bristol was thrown backward, his feet springing against the back cab before being thrust in the other direction. Without thinking about it, Bristol unlatched the back and quasi-somersaulted out of the bed. They were still in the woods, thankfully, so there was plenty of brush to hide under. JoJo and Stan didn't seem to notice anything amiss.

JoJo hopped out of the truck and continued down the worn grass path alone. Bristol swore softly, seeing his pace. He was counting on his silent walk to keep him inaudible, if not invisible, but the kid was booking it toward the town. Bristol was very careful just until he was sure he'd gotten out of Stan's range, but by then JoJo was out of sight. Bristol made his way to the path and ran.

He saw the ghost town before he saw JoJo. There was an abandoned gas station, with weeds blocking the pumps and the sign out front to the convenience store, though some of the letters were missing, so it now read "convenienc tor." Further in, there was a building that had once been something his mother would have called a strip mall. There were no houses. Bristol had seen pictures of these towns. In the old days before the uprising, people would drive cars from their homes to these places to get what they needed, then they'd fill those cars with gas and drive back home where little houses all stood in rows next to each other. Just next to, not on top of. *A total waste of vertical space*, Denver would say.

He'd lost JoJo, but he couldn't be far. The gas pumps were under an awning shaped like a "V," so Bristol climbed up and crunched down low on the roof. JoJo was easy to spot just a little farther ahead, bobbing up and down in a skip-like walk toward the far end of the strip mall. When he got to the farthest unit from Bristol, he stopped to knock at the door.

Bristol climbed down and ran alongside the back of the building. He didn't hear anything yet, and prayed he wouldn't. He didn't know what he would do if he heard any sign of violence—gunshots or screaming or anything like that—because come to think of it, he had nothing to defend JoJo or himself if he did.

Bristol was breathless when he got to the last unit, a small, narrow space with a largish plate glass window in front. The other windows were framed with jagged edges, having had their glass knocked down, but this one was pristine. He knelt down, took a deep breath, and raised his head to peer inside.

JoJo was in there, along with a woman who was pointing to stacks of cans and boxes. The woman wasn't just casually dressed; she looked slightly sloppy in her frayed black trousers and faded gray sweatshirt. When she pointed, her pit stain was clearly visible under the arm. JoJo was nodding. Bristol lowered and raised his head several more times until it looked like JoJo was asking the crucial question: he had his hand up by his face, one finger on his mouth. His foot slid in and out of his shoe, which was much too big for him. The woman shook her head from side to side. JoJo looked down at his shoe and the woman pulled him into a hug.

That's it, thought Bristol. *She might not be from the Red Sea, but she's not Metrics.* He darted around the corner just in time; the woman opened the front door and walked out into the parking lot where a shiny black singular transport stood parked.

Now to get back. Bristol had planned on walking back, taking all day if necessary to go back through the town and follow the path in the woods back to the monastery.

But he wasn't able to see that plan through. When he turned around to go back, he saw Stan's smiling face.

"I know you. You're one of us," he said.

Glancing down at the club in Stan's hand, Bristol thought it would be safer to tell the truth on that one. "Yes. I'm from St. Mary's."

"Don't know how you got here, but it's none of my business anyway. We'll just take you back with us."

Palpable relief washed over Bristol. "Thanks, man."

"Straight back," Stan continued. "To the leaders. It's none of my business, like I say. But they'll be curious."

CHAPTER TEN

DENVER DIDN'T SEE JOJO AGAIN UNTIL LUNCH.

"I'm sorry, Miss Denver. I couldn't get you...what your baby wanted."

"That's fine. Don't worry about it." She noticed his tray was shaking so much that drops of tinned pineapple juice were spilling onto it. "JoJo, is there anything else you need to tell me?"

"No?"

Denver looked at him curiously. "It sounds like there might be. Did they threaten you? I mean, did they say they would do bad things to you?"

"Not...them. Not to me."

Denver paused and studied him. His eyes, usually bright and crinkled under a smile, were large and searching. He wanted help, she could see, but wasn't asking for it. "JoJo..."

Stan stood up from his seat and put his hand on JoJo's shoulder. "I hope he's not bothering you, miss. Little man's been pestering everyone to help him with his math! What's sixteen divided by four, Jo?"

JoJo's shoulders dropped away from Stan's hand as he mumbled inaudibly.

"See? Kid's got no confidence. I'll help him, though—come on, Jo." Stan slapped him on the back with the same amount of force he'd use for an adult, and ignored the splash of juice this created on the floor.

Denver pulled a rag from her apron pocket and wiped up the spill. She looked up at JoJo, who had turned his head to face her again. He mouthed *Bristol.*

Bristol?

Denver told one of the ladies that she needed to go, and took off for the dorms. When she got to Bristol's, she burst in and scanned all the beds, unsure which was his. It didn't matter; he wasn't in any of them. She turned immediately, heart racing, and rushed to the meeting house.

She opened the doors and saw Samara and Taye both working with students at separate tables. "Oh, thank God," she breathed.

"Why?" asked Taye immediately.

Denver set a hard gaze on Taye and said, "I assumed I'd walk in on you two deep in a lover's embrace this time. I'm just thankful I didn't."

Taye smirked, but Samara stood up and walked to Denver, drawing her face close to hers. "What's wrong? Is it JoJo?"

"Maybe. Something does seem off. But I came to check on Bristol. Have you seen him?"

Samara's face fell. "No. Not since this morning when he said he was going to go talk to you."

"He told me he was going to bed."

"Then he didn't?"

"Of course he didn't," Denver snapped. "He went with JoJo, I'm almost sure of it now. Both JoJo and Stan acted like they were hiding something just now."

"Let's not do anything rash. Let's look some other places first. Ask Jude. Then, go look in his tree stand."

Denver nodded, then waited for Samara as she and Taye discussed him taking over for her for the rest of the day. Denver felt a bit silly waiting there for her, like a student herself, unsure of where to go and relying on a teacher to help. For much of her life, she had been a second mother to Bristol, especially after their father died and their mother needed all the help she could get. But her take-charge attitude was completely dependent on someone to take charge *of*, and Bristol had always provided that. With him missing, Denver could feel a bit of herself gone, too—in place of her assertiveness lay the meek and helpless child she scarcely remembered from the days her dad was still alive.

Denver and Samara didn't speak much as they ran out to look at Bristol's tree. When they got there, it was only Stephen and the other guard. Stephen wanted to come with them to look for Bristol, but Denver told him not to abandon his post; for all they knew, it was someone trying to sneak past the guards. She regretted this when she and Samara walked away, still not talking. Together, they checked the field, the infirmary, the lake behind the meeting house. There were no other options but to ask the leaders.

Samara looked at Denver. "I think it's best if you ask. They know that Bristol and I are in a relationship, but I don't think they'd approve."

Denver scowled. "They don't like romance. They keep me and Stephen apart, too."

"They don't want any trouble."

"Then maybe the time's right for a regime change."

Despite having been beside her for hours, Denver hadn't looked at Samara. She hadn't noticed the dried tear tracks down her cheek or cut on her lip where she'd been biting it. She noticed those now, and saw her face change to a brighter expression.

Samara moved toward her as if to give her a hug, but stopped short of that and patted her shoulder. "It's definitely time. Have you told the other girls in the kitchen?"

Denver's eyes widened. "No. No, I meant to after I talked with JoJo, but…"

"Never mind," said Samara. "Go tell them now, it's almost four and we have a group meeting at five. Then, everyone's going to bed. Make sure they know by the time they go to the meeting that they'll be waking up at eleven."

"What about Bristol?"

"I'll ask the leaders. We'll find them."

Denver nodded, wondering if she should offer something else to Samara—a handshake or a hug. But Samara immediately turned and ran toward the office, where Tommy, Karale, and Danovan spent most of their days.

Denver hadn't thought of how to tell the ladies she worked with that there would be a meeting to discuss overthrowing the leadership tonight. A part of her hoped she wouldn't have to do it, since it seemed like so much work to run from one society just to overthrow another. But Samara was right; something wasn't right here. Something had to be done before the leaders ushered in any more danger. She singled out the oldest woman first, who wasn't old but seemed to have lived long enough to have developed an air of authority. To Denver's surprise, the woman nodded vigorously when Denver asked if she ever had doubts about the leadership. The woman hung on Denver's every word as she explained the plan for later that night. After that discussion, they peeled away from each other and talked to as many women as they could while they prepared dinner. It was a curious thing, the kitchen staff talking to each other as they worked. The noise level didn't rise all that much, just a half-notch above the complete silence they'd come to expect as one woman talked to another in a whisper. By the time the line formed outside, to Denver's amazement, every member of the kitchen staff beamed, finally in the know.

Dinner was quick that evening—peanut butter sandwiches and applesauce—because everyone's attendance was required at the five o'clock meeting. Denver and the other kitchen workers hung their aprons on their designated hooks after cleanup and walked to the meeting house in a cluster.

Samara was sitting near the front of the crowd, and when she saw Denver walk in, she tried to mouth something to her, but Denver couldn't make it out without her contacts. Danovan walked to Samara and pointed at her chair. Samara gave Denver one last solemn look and sat.

Karale walked to the front of the room and onto the small stage. She raised her hands in the air, presumably to stop the chatter, but no one was chatting. She rolled her shoulders back. "Good evening! Thank you for coming. Tonight, we have an announcement. We've been lucky about the snow so far—it hasn't stuck to the ground, but there's always a chance it might. If this happens, we'll be stranded wherever we happen to be, as it's not worth the risk to create footprints. Currently, we have no one free to sweep them away after everyone who wants a little stroll!" She chortled in her throat, and Tommy and Danovan followed suit. "But seriously, we have a plan that will keep us all safer. Tonight, we'll begin a day-flip. We'll all wake up at midnight, and go to bed again when the sun rises. Going forward, we'll all pull the night shift until spring. Then, when there's no more chance of snow, we'll go back. This will make us all safer. Does anyone have any questions?"

Silence.

"Good! Now, speaking of safety—I don't want to alarm anyone, but there was a serious safety breach this morning."

She paused for a buzz and got one. People looked from face to face, whispering low. Karale held her hands up again.

"One of our own decided he wasn't satisfied with our meals that the hard-working kitchen staff provide us, so he went out in search of his own meal and very nearly ran into a Metrics official."

"Show 'em who it was!" called Danovan.

Denver's stomach dropped.

Tommy stood up and pulled someone up from the ground—Bristol, with a swollen lip and two black eyes, who struggled against Tommy as he shoved him onto the stage. People in the room began to gasp. Karale glared at him and took a tiny step away.

"Admit it," she said to him. "Admit that you put this entire community in danger with your selfishness."

Bristol croaked something, but Denver couldn't hear him. From the reaction of the first few rows, it was a confession. Denver's feet found the floor and she was halfway up before she realized what she was doing. *No,* she thought. *Sit down.* Karale was still rambling on about the dangers of selfishness and the consequences they could have faced if the leaders hadn't had the presence of mind to notice he was missing and heroically search for him.

A horrible thought hit Denver: *What if they know?* What if they were trying to instill some confidence in their abilities to keep the monastery safe? Maybe no one would show up to the secret meeting. Maybe they'd be too afraid.

"Denver Ray!" Karale nearly screamed, scanning the hall.

The woman next to Denver nudged her. "They want you to stand up."

Slowly, Denver stood.

"Here's our solution. Many of you don't know this, but Bristol here is Denver's brother. And Denver and her husband have put all of us in a different sort of danger: Denver is pregnant!"

Despite the atmosphere of fear, at the word "pregnant," applause broke out throughout the meeting house. Denver almost laughed, but forced the corners of her mouth down when she saw Karale's face.

"No! No!" Karale said. "Think about it! How can we be safe with a child around? The baby might delay our move! How would you like that? All this waiting and then having to wait more long months for a baby to make the trip with us?"

Silence again.

"We've given Bristol a choice. Either he can leave, or, when his sister's baby is born, *it* can." She turned again to Bristol. "What'll it be?"

"Me." Bristol's voice was booming and deep now.

"And *when* are you leaving, Bristol?" Karale's tone was taunting; this had obviously been discussed before.

"Now."

"No!" cried Denver. "They'll just take my baby anyway!"

Again, the hall came alive with whispers and murmurs.

Karale repeated "no" in little staccato punches, but Danovan, still on his chair, bellowed in a voice much too loud, "Quiet!"

He cleared his throat and looked at Denver. "You have our word. We make it to you in front of this entire assembly. You and your baby can stay together if your brother leaves."

His choice of words was not lost on Denver. *Can stay together,* not *can stay at St. Mary's.* She looked at Bristol, and then at Samara, who shook her head slightly. Denver sat down.

Karale turned back to Bristol. "If you want your sister and her baby to stay safe, you will not reveal our location to anyone unfortunate enough to meet you out there." She pointed to the door. "Now leave."

Tommy opened the door on the far side of the room, next to the stage. Danovan took Bristol by the back of his shirt and shoved him out. An icy blast swept into the room, and there was a collective shiver.

"Let's give him twenty minutes," said Karale, "and then we'll all get to sleep."

CHAPTER ELEVEN

Please, prayed Samara. *Please let him remember.*

They'd only talked it through once, the day they found this place. If, for whatever reason, one of them was in danger or they got separated, the little group—Bristol, Samara, Denver, Stephen, and Jude—would all meet up together on the side of the road where the car that drove them here first stopped. But Bristol's memory wasn't great, and it had been so long since they made that plan that Samara wasn't sure if it would work. Images of Bristol flashed in her head—Bristol being caught and beaten, Bristol alone and in the cold, Bristol lying face-down on the forest floor...

A tightening sensation seized Samara's lungs. She struggled to fill up with air, but her body refused to obey. She closed her eyes tight. Heat filled her, starting as a fire in the pit of her belly and spread into her limbs and face. She still couldn't breathe.

A pair of hands grasped her shoulders and led her onto the floor. Grateful for the wide surface, she crumpled and felt the cooler air on her face. She opened her mouth wide and drew in a breath. Better.

"A panic attack," a woman said from somewhere above her. "She needs to go to the infirmary."

The next voice she recognized as Taye's. "I'll take her."

Samara had a vague idea of protesting—she already felt better now that she could breathe—but Taye lifted her off the floor anyway and carried her out. Samara thought of Bristol turning back and having this be his last sight as he walked away. She thought of Denver watching from her chair in the back row. She wanted to say no and put her feet on the floor, but all of her energy was spent on breathing.

When they got to the infirmary, the little woman introduced herself as Nurse Sue and gave her bottle of water. While she was drinking, the nurse cleaned her arm and stuck a needle in before Samara knew what was happening. Samara sprang up into a fierce stance.

"What was that?" asked Samara.

"You had a panic attack, honey," said Nurse Sue. "It's no wonder. That poor boy..."

"Not that. What was in that?" Samara pointed to the syringe.

"This? It's just something to help you sleep. You can stay in here tonight. You both can, if you'd like." She nodded to Taye.

Samara had forgotten he was there. "He's not...we're not together."

"I can still stay with you and the nurse, just in case you need anything." Taye stood and took a step toward her.

Samara growled under her breath. "If I find out had you anything with this. Do. If I out find..." The first few words came out fine, but the others were slurred and unrecognizable, even to Samara's ears. "You..you..."

Nurse Sue nodded sympathetically and turned down the covers. She leaned down and whispered close to Samara's face, "If he's bothering you, he's out. Is he bothering you, honey?" Samara used her remaining presence of mind to nod. Taye left. Samara closed her eyes and heard the door shut. Nurse Sue still whispered, even though they were alone. "I'll stay with you here. Don't worry; someone's coming to tell me about the meeting later. We'll stay in the loop, you and me. You can sleep."

Samara closed her eyes but fought sleep until the light was off.
Then she opened her eyes as wide as physically possible and fought
more until she heard Nurse Sue's breathing change. By that time,
the clock on the shelf said 10:50. No longer able to be stealthy,
Samara tumbled out of bed and lumbered to the door. Nurse Sue
stirred but didn't wake, as far as Samara could tell. She made her
way to the meeting house, wondering all the way whether or not
she should turn back. Was she being too loud? She felt she might
slump over at any moment and spend the rest of the night on the
ground. *No. I'm going.* She put her chin down and stomped, one
slow foot in front of the other, all the way to the meeting
house door.

Stephen was there at the door. "Oh my God," he said when he
saw her. "Den? Help me with Samara."

Denver rushed over. She and Stephen took both of Samara's
arms and led her onto a chair, where she slumped over her legs,
breathing heavily. Samara tried to tell them about her injection,
but the words, directed at the floor, were still unrecognizable.

Denver propped her up and sat next to her so Samara could
lean on her shoulder. "They must have given her something. What
are we going to tell these people? She was the one with the plan."

Stephen licked his lips and looked around. "You'll just have to
wing it."

Denver looked incredulous. "Me?"

"Yes, you. Everyone knows you're pregnant now, and pregnant
women are equal parts vulnerable and ferocious. They'll listen
to you."

Samara silently agreed, even a little grateful that she didn't have
to confess to having no plan. As far as she could tell, Denver was
all ferocity and no vulnerability anyway.

When Samara woke again, she was back in the infirmary. The curtains on the windows were backlit with morning sunshine, though the air outside her blanket still felt chilly. Jude was there, leaned over a table where a thick book lay open. Samara sat up in bed, pleasantly surprised that she could still do so. Jude brightened.

"Hi, Miss Shepherd."

"Hi, Jude. What happened?"

As Jude's cheeks rose, so did his glasses and the top of his head with them. "We did it."

Samara closed her eyes to silently thank the universe. Jude continued, "I wasn't there, though. I just got back from the watch. But Denver asked me to tell her when you woke up." He scrambled up and out the door, leaving Samara alone with her wild curiosity and worries. What did he mean, exactly? Where was Bristol? Where were the leaders?

Denver walked in, followed closely by Stephen and Jude. Jude still wore his jubilant grin, but Denver and Stephen looked older and more tired than when she saw them last. Samara pelted them with her questions.

Denver simply sat on Samara's bed. "Move over," she commanded, and flopped down beside her like a rag doll. Samara, momentarily overwhelmed, looked from Denver to Stephen. Stephen threw up his hands and sat on the bed with them both.

"I don't know how much you remember," he said to Samara.

"Practically nothing."

"Well, Denver was great." He gave his wife's leg a little rub. "Right away, she got on stage but didn't like how that looked—like she was putting herself up as the new leader or something—so she stepped back down and asked everyone to put their chairs in a circle. To be honest, I thought it was a waste of time at first, since we only had fifty-five minutes at that point, but people did it quickly and the tone in the room changed after that, once people could see each other's faces. Then Denver said, 'The reason we're all here is because we have questions for the leaders, or we feel like we just need a new form of leadership. Which is it?' And people started raising two fingers in the air, like it was the second thing she said. And she just nodded and gave some options."

As grateful as Samara was that the meeting had gone well, she felt jealousy creeping in. Why hadn't she thought through this herself? "What were the options?"

"One, we could hold an election for one new leader. Just one person to make decisions for all of us. Two, we could elect representatives from each dorm to meet several times a week to strategize, then meet weekly with the big group to update us on the move to Canada. Three, we could talk to the current leaders to tell them that we need to know exactly what their ties are on the outside and strike on our work assignments until they agree to keep us better informed."

"What did they choose?"

"Well, they liked the third idea, but the idea of striking hurts the whole group. We could all deal with things not being as clean as usual for a while, but someone has to keep watch, someone has to feed us. We could go without food for a little while, but if they informed their contact that there was a coup, we might not get any food for the foreseeable future. So, in the end, they decided on Number Two. We elected representatives from the dorms."

"And where—"

"Karale and Danovan and Tommy are locked in the youth dorm. We moved the kids into the dorms with us. We've got people guarding them, and Taye's interrogating them. We still need to know where their ties are, and how deep. They've admitted to communicating with people on the outside, but they won't say whether it's Metrics or someone else."

"We think it's the Red Sea," said Jude.

"But they won't say that," added Stephen.

"Why not? Why wouldn't they want us to know that?" asked Samara.

"Because," said Stephen, "they don't want us to go looking for help. They may have made a deal with the Red Sea, promised to keep us safe for a while, and don't want us to undermine the relationship."

"Keep us safe until when?" asked Samara.

"These are questions we don't have answers to. We have to wait until they tell us, or until we figure it out. We're working on it. We think JoJo knows a bit more than he thinks, or maybe he just doesn't know how to say it. He's only seven."

"I could try to talk to him," said Jude. "You know, ask him if he knows where the food lady is from, if he knows who the Bird is. For the things he doesn't know, I could put together a list of questions for her the next time he meets with her. I could even rehearse with him."

"Good idea, Jude." Samara turned back to Stephen. "One more question."

"Bristol's still missing." They were the first words Denver had spoken since she walked in. "We had to coax JoJo a little, but he told the group that he knew Bristol was innocent. But he wouldn't say how he knew. We were hoping he'd come back to see what happened after our meeting."

"But he hasn't yet?"

"No."

Something suddenly occurred to Samara. "Which way did they take him?"

"South. Toward the road," said Denver. "The leaders told us that right away."

Stephen realized it, too. He stood up. "Oh my God."

"They led him toward the lasercams." said Samara.

"Which aren't just weapons."

"They're cameras." Samara's heart quickened. "Our location has been compromised. We're not safe here."

CHAPTER TWELVE

JUDE LISTENED AS SAMARA, STEPHEN, AND DENVER strategized. They decided to act immediately: first, Stephen went to question the leaders about Bristol's location. Tommy confessed to sending Bristol into the laser cam line of fire right away, then turned white after a glance at the horrified expressions on the faces of Karale and Danovan. After that, the three former leaders bickered about whose fault it was that they were now in danger and wouldn't allow themselves to be interrupted.

Denver turned to Jude as the shouting grew louder. "Jude, we need you to go get JoJo. Take him to a quiet place where he feels safe and get any information you can. Come back to us right away when you think you have anything at all. Metrics may already be on their way."

Jude left, relieved and reeling from what this place did to ordinary people. On the outside, people didn't shout at each other —they barely even had arguments. With the watches they'd worn that tracked their every move—and probably most of their words —and told them where to be and when, they'd never had the opportunity to fight it out. All you'd had to do was to enter the situation into an application and Metrics would tell you who was right and who was wrong. Here, everything was so different, so gray...he never fully appreciated how difficult it would be to run a country. Ruling themselves was threatening to end in disaster. He wondered if this was why the uprising happened in the first place —if a similar catastrophic exercise in democracy was the reason Metrics existed at all.

He found JoJo with a few other boys and gratefully realized that he knew at least one of them—Cork. They were passing around a shrinking cigarette. Jude had his marching orders and no intention of wasting time, but Cork stood and gestured toward himself.

"He's had a hard night, man." Cork spoke in a hushed register. "He blames himself for what happened to that guy. If your friends want to see him, ask if they can wait until he sleeps a little."

The space between Jude's brows shortened. "It can't wait. But they don't want to see him. Just me. I need to ask him some questions and then go back. You can stay if you want, if you think it'll make him more comfortable."

Cork straightened his back and glanced back at the huddle of little men. "Henry is his best friend. Let Henry stay, and we'll all go. I think you'll get the best answers that way."

With a silent gesture, Cork directed all the other boys back inside the dorm and left Jude alone on the stoop with JoJo and Henry.

"He don't know nothin' but what he already told ya," said Henry.

"That may be true," he said, "But I'd like to help him remember anything he may not." He turned to JoJo. "Metrics might know about this place and we all might be in danger right now."

JoJo and Henry exchanged rattled looks. JoJo wiped his nose with the back of his hand while Henry put out the cigarette. "What do you want to know?" asked JoJo. His eyes were red and swollen and his seven-year-old voice held the drudge of the cigarette.

"Who is the lady you met with?"

JoJo held his gaze down and coughed. Jude reached for his thermos attached to his belt and offered it to him.

"What's that?" JoJo asked.

"Just hot water. It'll make your throat feel better."

The little boy took a long drink, then wiped his lips with the back of his hand. "Her name is Miss Gwen."

"Why do you meet with her?"

"She gives us food."

"How does she have all that food to give?"

"It's not her food. It's Canada's food."

"The food is from Canada?"

"The food, the water, the protection, everything. Miss Gwen says the gumin gives us what we need, and they're coming to get us and bring us to Canada, and then it'll be our gumin, too."

"Government? The Canadian Government is supporting us?"

"That's what he just said," interjected Henry.

Jude decided to ignore him. "What about the Red Sea?"

"The what?"

Jude drew in cold air and studied JoJo's face. Nothing. "Never mind. Tell me everything the leaders told you to do when they gave you this job, okay?"

"Okay." JoJo sniffled. "I was in laundry, but then Danovan got hurt and couldn't do this job anymore. He was the one who used to go into town, but Metrics shot at him and made his arm bleed. Then he didn't want to do it anymore, so he asked me. I thought it sounded like fun, but I didn't want to get shot and bleed, so I started crying. Danovan told me, 'Hold on, wait a second,' and then he got something out of his desk drawer, and it was a real gun. And he said, 'If you don't do this job, I'll make you bleed here.' I couldn't help it; I cried more. But I said okay, I'll do it. But that was the only scary part—Miss Gwen is nice and she even made the gumin change towns so I didn't have to go to the place where they shot Danovan."

"Does Miss Gwen ever tell you when they'll come get us?"

"No. She just says, 'Soon, baby,' and then she gives me a hug." JoJo's eyes were suddenly wet. "She's going to get worried if I don't go meet her. Do I still get to keep my job?"

Jude wanted to be honest, but he needed answers, not a meltdown. He tried to answer JoJo like Samara would. "Of course you do. Now, what happened with Bristol?"

"Him? I just went back to the car and Mister Stan had him tied up with rope. He sat between Mister Stan and me, so he couldn't jump out of the car. I asked why would he jump out, since he's all tied up and he'd just bounce? Mister Stan said shut up, he didn't know what this guy was doing but it probably wasn't good. But Bristol looked at me and he didn't look like he was a bad guy. I'm pretty good at telling who the bad guys are."

"Yeah, you get good at that here. Is Mister Stan a bad guy?"

"No, he's not. He's just a scared guy. Like me." JoJo covered his face with his hands. "I wanted to tell Mister Stan not to tell Danovan, but Danovan told me he'd make me bleed if I told anyone about the gun too. Then when we saw Bristol again, he *was* bleeding. It's my fault."

JoJo sobbed. Henry's jaw quivered as he surveyed his friend. Jude wished he had cigarettes of his own to offer. He remembered what JoJo said about Miss Gwen. Jude had only been hugged by one person in his life—Samara—but he remembered that it felt nice, so he decided to try it now. He put an awkward arm around JoJo's back and patted his head with the other hand. It definitely didn't feel right, but it seemed to calm JoJo down, or perhaps confuse him enough to make the crying stop.

"One more question," said Jude. "And if you know, it's important that you tell me now. Who is the Bird?"

"That's another man. He's not here, but I don't think he's a Canada person either."

"What makes you think that?"

"I only saw him once, when Miss Gwen wanted to change the town we met in. He was an old guy, and he wore a watch. I don't think they do that in Canada."

Jude drew his arms back, looked up into the sky, and groaned.

"What's that?" asked JoJo.

"Snow."

CHAPTER THIRTEEN

BRISTOL FOUND A LOW TREE WITH BRANCHES THAT LOOKED TO provide a sort of umbrella, so he ducked under it. He'd heard the name 'weeping willow' once and thought it was a magnificent name, but this didn't seem to be one. He'd only seen a picture in one of Denver's books, a sprawling monster that didn't look like it was weeping at all, but seemed to sit lavishly, enjoying the space it was taking for its own. The tree he sat under now was squat, almost a bush. But Bristol didn't need luxury right now. He need a reason to stop and think, and a place to do it. Now Nature had given him both.

From the moment Tommy began leading him toward the lasercams, Bristol had decided to go with him as far as Tommy would dare to go, then find a place to wait until morning. The only thing that had worried him was his certainty that Tommy would lead him all the way to the road, and wouldn't turn back until he was sure Bristol had been zapped. But he'd turned out to be a coward as well as a fool—he'd merely pointed Bristol in the direction of the road, given him a spiteful little push, and run away. Thinking fast, Bristol had stumbled forward, hoping to project helplessness, and then run toward the lasercam himself and thrown

a rock in its direction. He'd heard the shock of the laser ring
through the woods, and Bristol had hit the ground, hoping Tommy
would report back that his plan had worked.

Now, hours later, as Bristol watched the snow smother the
ground below, he realized it wouldn't be wise to travel back now,
leaving tracks behind in the sunlight. He hoped the group stuck to
the decision to switch days and nights, so they'd be safe inside if
any drones flew overhead.

While Tommy had prodded him toward the line of lasercams—
the dolt—Bristol had looked back to catch a startling image: a man
carrying Samara. She seemed to be conscious, which was a good
sign, but why did she allow herself to be carried at all? It wasn't like
her. Samara had a teacher's heart, a caretaker's spirit, so she
wouldn't just allow herself to be carried at the drop of a hat
unless...unless...

Denver's warnings of mistrust rang through his memory.
Samara had been off night-watch duties for more than a week now,
and Bristol still had only vague ideas of what life was like on
campus for people who had day shifts. What if she was getting
friendly with this guy? They hadn't talked much since she'd
changed positions, but she had said there was another teacher
working with her and conspicuously failed to mention the gender
of this teacher. At the time, Bristol had thought it would seem
stupid and jealous to ask. Now he wished he had risked being
stupid and jealous.

More snow fell to the earth in large chunks. Bristol's
exhaustion consumed him and made him pant. He hadn't slept in
over twenty-four hours, and if he didn't get some sleep on his own
terms soon, he'd drift away and fall victim to hypothermia before
he found out what happened in the group. He got up, found a
place in the sun, and cleared away leaves until he unearthed a small
patch of ground. He gathered some rocks from the nearby stream
and arranged them in a circle, then worked to light a fire with two
sticks.

As he worked and looked for sparks, his mind stayed with

Samara. Come to think of it, they really hadn't talked much about their relationship since they were taken in at St. Mary's. Bristol had thought that was nice back then; he thought in pictures rather than words anyway—pictures were so much more useful for explaining what you really meant, unlike words, which meant so many different things to different people. He'd waited for the first chance he got—the first time they were alone had been their first night watch shift together. They'd walked into the forest, and he'd taken her hand. He'd felt her change at just his touch, like water turning to steam. He'd kissed her deeply while she'd slid her hands under his shirt and caressed his back. Without a word, they'd knelt together on the forest floor. He'd been clumsy and graceless, but Samara hadn't even seemed to notice. She made him feel like something precious; someone chosen. She'd pulled at him until her breaths had become gulps. He'd tried to back away from her then, to stop her pain, but she'd just drawn him closer.

After that, they'd discussed what a foolish idea it had been, however magnificent. They hadn't wanted to be split up, but the leaders had made it clear that romance was discouraged and that couples would not be allowed to be alone together. They'd just pretended to be platonic in public and snuck affection when they could. And that was the last time they'd spoken about their relationship. That had been six months ago.

Bristol shivered. Still no fire, but he kept trying. When he was on the night watch, Bristol wore his long underwear, wool socks, several layers of shirts, his big hunting coat, gloves, and a thick toboggan that covered his ears. He'd removed his coat and hat to talk to Denver this morning. That conversation seemed like it was months ago. The temptation to turn the bitter cold into bitter thoughts about himself for leaving his outerwear back in his dorm was strong, but he reminded himself that Tommy likely would have taken them anyway. Why not take the chance that he'd freeze to death?

Finally, the smallest of sparks appeared and grew into a meager flame. He worked a while longer to keep it going. The line of smoke rising into the sky, weak and wispy as it was, presented a risk, but Bristol took it, gathered leaves around himself, and fell asleep.

He woke as the sun was setting. His muscles ached from their constant tension, but Bristol barely noticed—his joy at waking up at all overwhelmed him. He scrambled to his feet and put out the embers of his fire, walked the stones back down to the stream, and when the dark covered the land again, he set off in what he hoped was the direction of the monastery.

He walked for a long time without knowing for sure where he was going. True, he was only here the night before, and they hadn't changed directions many times, but Bristol might as well have been a different person back then—his body's need for sleep and recovery from his injuries was enough to overwhelm him, but then there was this question of Samara in the man's arms as well. He'd been useless to his future self last night, not that he could have even been sure that there would be a future self for him to watch out for. He felt much better now, and assured himself that Samara would have an explanation for him when he returned. He stopped for a moment to compose himself.

There was a funny sound behind him—a sound he'd never heard before. Like a growl low in someone's throat.

He turned slowly. What he saw shocked him—an animal. A wild animal.

It was about the size of a dog, though it was not like any of the dogs he'd seen roaming the streets, and grayish, with a long nose and teeth that Bristol could see even though they were relatively far away from each other. They stood staring at each other, man and beast, for what seemed like a long time before the wheels in Bristol's mind began turning. He heard a small voice inside say *run,* and only then did he realize that he was afraid.

Another one appeared, this one slightly larger and browner.

Bristol stared at him, too. They were so far, though, and Bristol needed to get a closer look. He took a small step toward them. The animals took a step back. *They're afraid of me,* thought Bristol. No wonder. He was sure that, at some point, his species had tried to murder theirs.

Two more of them appeared on either side of the two that were already there, and together, they began to advance, all of them making that noise and showing teeth. Now the voice in Bristol's head was a little stronger: this time, it said *climb.* He lunged for a tree in front of them as they ran to catch him. One of them got its mouth around Bristol's boot and threatened to drag him down, but Bristol kicked—in self-defense or in an effort to get up the tree, or maybe both—and the animal yelped and let go. This tree wasn't a good one for climbing—there were no branches for a long way up, so Bristol had to clutch with his arms and legs wrapped around the truck. He shimmied up another few feet, making his forehead sticky with sweat. He looked down at the animals, still there beneath him. Several more had arrived to support their brethren. Bristol groaned. He had no food, no water, nowhere to rest. He threw back his head and roared Samara's name into the forest.

CHAPTER FOURTEEN

SAMARA PACED BACK AND FORTH, WAITING FOR TAYE TO EMERGE from the dorm where the three former leaders were being held. They'd figured he was the best person to talk to them, as he and Denver were the only other Threes in here, and Denver hadn't gotten anywhere with her questions.

When he finally did walk out the door, he moved toward Samara with intention. He had a look that suggested he wanted to embrace her, but he did not. Instead, he pulled at his jaw and stared at the ground.

"I know you don't want to believe it, but the truth is that there's only a small chance that Bristol has survived," he said. "I'm sorry, but we have to move quickly."

"Absolutely. I'll put together the search party." Samara turned to get to work, but Taye caught her arm.

"No," he said. "That's not what I mean. Listen, Tommy fully admits he's at fault—though with Karale and Danovan screaming at him like that, he was unlikely to say anything else—but he says he heard a lasercam go off when he was walking away."

Samara was quiet for a moment. "Did he see Bristol die?"

"He didn't say."

"Bristol's tougher than you think," Samara said. "You think just because he's Unregistered—"

"That's not what I think at all! My own brothers are Unregistered!" He was still holding her forearm. "I only went in there to talk to them as Threes because that's what *they* care about. That's not what I care about. I know there are more important things than Tier, there always were, but they're *more* important here than they ever were on the outside." He let go of her arm, but she kept it held out. "Tommy may have murdered your boyfriend, but he also endangered all of us here. We can only do something about one of those. If Bristol is alive, then he has to do his part and find us. We have to get everyone out tonight."

Samara was surprised to hear the word *tonight.* "Now? What did they tell you?"

"They told me that they did have a contact with Metrics. An old man, kind of a crazy old man, who has been in Metrics since the uprising. He helped write the articles of the new constitution and everything. He's an idealist, though, and they say he sees that Metrics hasn't lived up to his vision. But he's also kind of crazy— he doesn't have a Tier, since none of the founders gave themselves Tiers, but the people he works with are all Ones. They don't understand why he isn't a One, and they do nothing but mock and belittle him."

"But he's a founder. The founder of the whole system that benefits them!"

"They're blinded by power. He's technically Unregistered himself, so that's how they treat him. Apparently, he's been helping the Red Sea for years and has gotten hundreds of people across the border."

"How?"

"I think we should go join the others before I tell you." He cracked a half-smile. "That's the important part."

They rushed to the infirmary, where the new leaders were still meeting to strategize. Among them were Denver, Stephen, Nurse

Sue, and a few other men whom Samara had never met before.
Nearly all of them stood when they saw Taye approaching.

"Well?" asked Stephen.

Taye told them what he knew about the Bird, then went on to
tell them about the old man who had been cooperating with the
Canadian government to smuggle Unregistered citizens across the
border that none of them had known existed until very recently.
"The Red Sea used to have safe houses along a route, and there
were paths to follow to each one. At the last one, they'd wait until
they had enough people to load onto a bus, then take them across
on this little dirt road where they wouldn't be seen. They think
with the relocation, the safe houses were all destroyed"—here
Samara gulped as she listened—"and the bus they used may have
also been damaged. It suggests Metrics knew about the Red Sea
network for quite some time, but never did anything about it."

"What' a missing Unreg here and there?" Samara murmured,
repeating the words she heard on her first night in Nan's
safe house.

"That seems like their attitude, yes," Taye said. "But
Unregistered numbers were growing, and they couldn't send all
Unregs to Canada, or else they ran the risk of the Registered
citizens finding out that other countries existed."

"So they decided to kill them, and tell the Registered that
they'd been relocated," Stephen said. "Well, we knew all that. Did
Metrics connect the old man to the Red Sea?"

"Karale doesn't think so. The Bird was the one who set up the
support system with the Canadian government, so he wouldn't be
able to do that if they were on to him."

"Does anyone know—the Bird or the Canadians or whatever—
that we need to run again?"

"Not yet. If we choose to, we've got the Bird's contact
information. We can ask for help. Remember, we're the leaders
now."

Nearly everyone in the room looked at the floor. Samara let
this revelation wash over her as well. It had been comforting living

in Metrics, even as a Five. To never have to worry about surviving, to be safe and free from worry about the future, was something she'd taken for granted. She longed for that security back. She looked up and inadvertently caught the eye of Denver.

Denver cleared her throat and lifted her chin. "We need to find Bristol first."

The room was silent. Samara could sense, as one of the few people in the room who had experience in the world of multiple Tiers, the Unregistered in the room searching for the courage to contradict her. Finally, one of the men found it.

"No," he said. "I think need to let the Bird know now. I'm very sorry. I'm very sorry." He repeated his last sentence, acknowledging both Denver and Samara.

The others in the room murmured their agreement with the Unregistered man, a tall and broad-shouldered guy who suddenly seemed to have been born a leader. Under different circumstances, Samara realized that, at one point in her life, she would have agreed with him as well and felt good about doing it. But she had learned too much, seen too much, to revert back to that.

"We are all here," said Samara quietly, "because Metrics decided that our lives were, for one reason or another, not worth saving. That we or someone we loved was not worth the financial costs, or that our knowledge made us a risk to society. We don't have to be perfect, but we do need to be better than that."

"I agree," said Stephen immediately. "We can't leave Bristol. We can't leave anyone."

Taye looked around. "Samara and I weren't elected leaders. You all were. You need to vote on what to do now." He looked to Samara. "And we need to respect their decision. This is what we wanted."

It wasn't even close. Taye went back to the old leaders to tell them, and the new leaders began rushing to write a message to the Bird.

While they were huddled together suggesting ways to tell him what had happened, Stephen looked from Denver to Samara and gave a little nod toward the door. Samara didn't understand—was he trying to get rid of her? But Denver took her by the hand and led her out the door.

The wind whipped Samara's face. "What are we doing?"

"What do you think, stupid?" The corners of Denver's mouth twitched upward as she tightened her scarf. "We're going to find my brother."

CHAPTER FIFTEEN

JUDE COULDN'T HIDE HIS SURPRISE WHEN BRISTOL CAME LIMPING toward his stand. He gave a little yelp of shock and relief, and even though he never really got the impression that Bristol liked him at all, when Jude lumbered down the tree and toward him, Bristol caught his shoulders and pulled him into an embrace. Jude immediately stiffened, but patted him with his good hand several times before breaking away.

"You're supposed to go back to the road where our car stopped," Jude said, more of a statement of surprise that he was not there already than an accusation. "Samara said they were going to send a search party to go find you there."

"Oh—" Bristol's face suggested that he'd forgotten. Jude, elated to have discovered something unsaid in another human being's expression, trembled with excitement and possibility.

"But maybe they haven't sent the search party yet!" he said. "They're talking about what to do now that we have to leave."

"Leave?" Bristol asked.

"Yeah, well—didn't the lasercams see you?"

"If they had, I wouldn't be here." Bristol briefly explained how he'd thrown a stick to catch a laser, but that Metrics would probably think it was just a falling branch, if they'd seen it at all. "Or maybe they'll think it was a forest animal."

"What?" Jude's eyes widened as he listened to the story of the animals with the gray-brown coats and the sharp teeth. "Cool!"

"Well, not so cool. One of them bit me. I should really get back and get this cleaned up, but I got lost. I'm glad I found you."

Jude beamed and let that word sink in—*you*, not a generic *somebody*.

Bristol kept talking about his injury and how his arms ached from hanging onto the tree trunk, but Jude interrupted him with a quiet *shh*. Someone was coming. It would take him too long to climb back up, and Bristol wasn't in any shape to get to his usual branch either, so both of them hid behind a tree and listened to the quiet, almost silent, footsteps get closer. Jude could tell they were coming from the direction of the monastery, but with all of the uncertainty going on there, he couldn't be sure it was a friend approaching.

Jude heard Stephen's distinctive cough just before he heard him call his name. "Jude?"

Jude lunged out to him. "I'm here!" He pointed to Bristol. "And look who else is here!"

Bristol and Stephen shook hands with broad smiles; both suddenly seemed very tall. Jude felt himself shrinking. "He forgot about the plan."

"I did. The search party hasn't gone out yet, has it?"

Stephen frowned. "The new leadership decided—"

"To let me go." Bristol shook his head. "I knew it."

"Well, yes, but ponder what that says about human behavior later. Samara and Denver did go on their own, and they weren't back when I left. I came to get Jude because the Canadians are here with their airship. They're taking us away."

"We can't leave without Miss Shepherd," asserted Jude, not realizing at first that he'd used Samara's teacher name.

"Or Denver," said Bristol.

"Of course not. But they may be back already."

"Without having found me? Are you crazy? Do you *know* Samara and Denver?"

Bristol had a point. Jude wasn't as close to Denver, but he couldn't imagine Samara giving up on anyone. She'd risked her comfortable life to save Jude, but he had a suspicion that she and Bristol had a connection that he didn't quite understand. Whatever it was, it would compel her deeper into the forest, not back the way she came.

"I'm going to find them," said Jude.

"The airship is there now—they're already loading us in. And they can't wait forever. There's a very good chance we could be stuck here with no support if we don't go."

Bristol balked. "My sister is carrying your child. You'd just leave them here, as long as you can get to safety?"

"Of course not. I'm suggesting that I go find them, and you two get back as quick as you can."

Jude shook his head wildly and Bristol shouted "No!" Stephen threw up his hands—*have it your way*—and, turning away from Bristol and Jude, began to walk north. Jude glanced at Bristol, and the two of them followed.

Soon enough, Jude heard a crunching of leaves, not the kind of sound two women who'd relearned how to walk quietly would make, nor the kind he imagined animals would allow. A boisterous sound, like whoever was walking thought they weren't in the woods at all, but in their own bedroom, safe on the outside, where no one worried about who might be watching them.

There was no time at all to run or hide—five or six men in military uniforms came barreling through the forest until one of them pointed to the three of them and called out a greeting in a cheery voice. All the soldiers, who were dressed like soldiers and moved like soldiers, were all suddenly very un-soldier-like, throwing up their arms and shouting in celebration. The one who called out came running. Jude widened his stance slightly, feet gripping the insides of his boots.

"Thought we'd never find you!" the soldier said.

"Well, now, that's a lie now, ain't it?" said another, then turned to Stephen, the tallest of the three. "We wouldn'ta left you here."

"Why d'ya look like you've seen a ghost?" the first asked with a laugh.

Jude's mind went wild with answers, and he began blurting them out before he knew what he was saying. "Because you're so loud! And you sound—I can understand you, but you sound so..." He realized he didn't know how to finish.

"Ah," said one solider to the other four. "They haven't heard a proper English accent before."

"That's not a proper one, mate. He's a Brummy."

Jude felt his mind struggling with the new sounds. What a strange thing, to understand, yet a fraction of a second behind what it was used to processing. Bristol looked at Stephen, who looked as confused as Jude felt.

"Wait a minute," said Stephen. "We were told that the Canadians were coming for us."

"Technically, they did. The United Kingdom is their ally. Your government is keeping a closer eye on them, so we jolly old Brits are picking you up instead."

"Sorry about that," said another soldier, and the others laughed.

"We don't have to be quiet; there's no one around for miles. But we do have to be fast. C'mon; let's go."

"We're waiting for—"

"The ladies? Already found 'em, mate. All we're waiting on is you three buggers."

Jude tried to keep the corners of his mouth from curling up, but they wouldn't stop. It had been so long since he'd heard talk like this, light and good-natured. Bristol seemed to be having the same problem with his mouth.

"Let's go," he said with frown that was struggling to stay a frown.

St. Mary's was barely recognizable with the gargantuan black airship parked on the field. It was another funny contrast, and

Jude's eyes struggled to take it all in: he'd never seen an airship on the ground before, and it looked much larger than they did in the sky. The black paint gleamed against the snow on the decaying grass and shabby cabins. The jovial soldiers gave them special blankets made of crinkly material which managed to keep them warm nonetheless. The campus had an eerie atmosphere, a silence different from the usual silence of people keeping mostly to themselves. At least then it was moderately alive, as the Unregistered were used to living their lives. With no one around at all, it was ghostly.

The airship lowered down a wide ramp and Jude followed Bristol and Stephen inside. Both Stephen and Bristol hiked up the ramp and immediately whipped their heads from left to right, looking, Jude supposed, for Samara and Denver. Jude got one short glance inside—a large flat surface, black all over, with campers wrapped in their blankets and huddled along the walls of the airship—before the soldiers ran in behind them and made a silent motion. Immediately, the ramp snapped shut and plunged the inside of the airship into darkness.

There was a hand at his elbow, and a soldier said, "Just sit down where you are, mate. It's a fast take-off."

Jude sat, and his stomach dropped as they were lifted straight into the air at a speed he'd never felt before. It was a few seconds before he realized he was holding his breath. He took in a long drink of air and wondered for a moment if they were still moving. The hand at his elbow slapped at his shoulder.

"Cool, innit?"

Jude didn't know how to respond. He reached his good hand out for Bristol, swatting in the dark until something crinkled. "Bristol!" he whispered.

"I'm here, Jude." Bristol's voice was low and serious.

"Where are Samara and Denver?"

Silence.

"I said, where are—"

"I heard you. I don't know."

Now Jude was silent as he struggled not to cry. "What are we going to do?"

"We're going to have faith."

"Faith?" Jude's voice cracked, but he no longer cared how small he sounded. "What's that?"

Bristol's hand bounced against his own, and enveloped it firmly. "Hoping, even when you have no reason to hope."

"Is that all?"

"That's all."

CHAPTER SIXTEEN

DENVER GOT ONE SHORT GLANCE OF STEPHEN AND BRISTOL entering the airship before all the lights went out. She took off her coat and backpack for the first time and placed them both on Samara's lap. "Hold these for me," she whispered and crawled in Stephen's direction. She groped in the black air for him. "Stephen?"

She heard a sob, and a moment later, while her mind worked to put together who this might be—the voice sounded older than a child's—she felt the unmistakable touch of her husband's hand on her hand, then her wrist, then her arm. He pulled her toward him and sobbed again, and the cries became wild, unconscious manifestations of what she herself was feeling—relief. Disbelief of their own luck. They held each other in a tight embrace. It no longer mattered that they couldn't see. Even without touching each other for weeks, Denver knew this body like she knew her own, as if she'd already spent an entire lifetime holding it.

His warm tears wet her lips when she kissed him. "I thought you might be still..."

"They came and found us."

With effort, he exhaled. "Bristol and Jude are here."

"Thank you. Thank you."

"Don't thank me; I didn't do anything."

"I'm not thanking you, exactly. I'm thanking...whatever it is, the thing we can't see, whatever's helping us."

"Something we can't see is helping us?" Stephen snickered. "Tell it to try harder."

"Stephen, we're still alive. And our baby is growing, even after all this. *Something* is helping us."

"Maybe. I'd say it was crazy if you weren't really here." He put his hand on her belly. "Both of you."

They didn't say much more for the rest of the journey. Denver laid her head on Stephen's lap and dozed off. She stopped counting how many times she drifted in and out of consciousness. It was hard to tell anyway, with the loud shushing noises of the airship and the darkness dulling her senses. She woke up for good when she heard a magnified voice in that funny accent.

"Ladies and gentlemen, we're sorry to keep you in the dark for so long, but we didn't want anyone catching a glimpse of our cargo." He paused while two or three people—Denver suspected Brits—gave a polite chuckle. "But we're safely in Scotland now, so we'll open up the windows in just a moment to give you a glimpse of your new home. Enjoy!"

"Scotland?" Denver asked softly and immediately brought her hand to her face to shield her from the blinding light. She blinked and slowly turned to look out the window behind her.

It was amazing, breathtaking. Gray and green, grounding shades against brilliant ones, filled her vision and she gaped at the hills, the tiny buildings, the clouds that appeared closer than they ever had before. There was no reason to expect that she'd ever fly on an airship, since she wasn't employed in the military or anything, so she'd had no time to prepare for this experience. She'd spent so much time hardening herself, which normally prepared herself for experiences that might come close enough to her heart to touch it, but she hadn't prepared for this. Hill and sky so beautiful that they couldn't be possible.

The landing was light, especially for such a monster of a machine. The magnified voice filled the space again: "Thanks for flying with us. A couple of announcements before you step off. One, please make sure to take all personal belongings, including your space blanket. There's, eh...quite a crowd outside. Mostly they just want to offer their support to you and offer you luck on your journey. But if you're asked a question, don't answer it."

Denver looked at Stephen. "They should have met with us first to tell us this," she said in an attempt to knit together a few shreds of old dignity. "We're the leaders here."

"We're not, baby. Not any more than they are." He gestured over to Karale, Danovan, and Tommy, who huddled together clutching their blankets to their shoulders, looking as frightened and confused as everyone around them. "We had to make the call that we did, we had to get help, but we sacrificed something to do it."

Samara walked over, holding Denver's coat and backpack out to her. In this pristine platform, she could finally smell the rottenness on it. She reached out anyway and tucked them under her blanket. Bristol and Jude walked over too.

"Forgot to go to the road, huh?" she said to Bristol.

"If you really knew me, you wouldn't have even bothered to check. What kind of sister are you, anyway?"

Denver was going to tell him that she was at least a living one, no thanks to him, but the words got stuck in her throat. Instead, she reached out and gave Bristol a little punch on the arm. He started to return it, but stopped when the hatch of the ship began to open and they heard roar of the crowd.

Later, Denver could barely remember being escorted from the ship. Her senses had been overloaded with new faces in different colors with rowdy sounds and funny phrases coming out of every one. She could hardly piece together how she knew where they were going, that a nice lady with a chunky pink sweater with little white hairs on it had sat beside her and told her that they were going to stay in the Olympic

Village until World United had sorted out their refugee paperwork.

"We hosted the Olympics here in Edinburgh just a few years ago. We're all so happy that all those buildings won't go to waste."

It took Denver a few beats to understand what the woman meant. "What are the Olympics?" she finally asked.

The woman just got tears in her eyes, patted Denver's hand, and walked away to inform the next row where they were going.

At the Olympic Village, there were more volunteers, this time in crisp cotton scrubs, to take them to their rooms—Denver and Stephen were allowed to share one—and give them shower supplies. The bathroom was connected to their own room, just like a home. She hadn't had a shower in months—at the monastery, on the rare occasion they had soap, they just did their best with the sink. Stephen insisted that she go first.

She turned on the water and played with the temperature. When it was close to scalding, she got in, shocked at first at how sensitive she was to the sensation of water hitting her skin. Months of enduring the cold, of carrying a putrid backpack under her coat, of not smiling, finally caught her. She allowed the pleasure of hot water on her skin to fill her with life, and, digging her fingers into her matted hair and breathing in steam, she wept.

They said everyone needed to see the doctor, but they made Denver wait longer to see a specialist. Smiling men in scrubs herded Jude away with the other kids, but no one seemed to mind the fact that Stephen, Bristol, and Samara stayed with her, waiting together.

Not even the doctor seemed to mind. When he arrived and Denver introduced him to everyone, he waved them all into the exam room and patted the stretcher. Denver sat on it while he asked his questions.

"What was the date of your last period?"

These accents were very disorienting. "My what?"

"Period."

Denver looked at Stephen, who looked back blankly. The doctor scratched his nose. "When did you last bleed?"

Denver glanced at the scrape on her right hand, wondering if the tree she'd brushed the night before had drawn blood. The doctor saw it and gently took her hand. "That doesn't look so bad," he said. "What I'm asking is—when did you last bleed from inside?"

Something clicked, but Denver did her best to pretend it hadn't. "Oh—the period. The date was...November tenth." Probably not the exact date, but close.

The doctor smiled and took a paper wheel from his pocket, twisting it. Denver eyed the wheel. These were the kinds of tools they tried to avoid back on the outside. She gave herself an internal shake—she guessed she was on the outside again, just a different outside. In the USA, she meant, tools that were somehow both chunky and flimsy were looked down upon. They could always just project a hologram when they needed everyone in the room to see some information. She noticed he wasn't wearing a watch.

"Your baby is due on August sixteenth. You're about eleven weeks along." He took out another tool, a little wand made from plastic, with a springy little cord on the end. "Let's listen to the heartbeat."

He pointed the wand on her belly. The machine made a loud shushing noise. Denver stared at her belly. She had only a small notion that a little person was in there at all. She saw the doctor smile before she heard what he heard: a rhythmic pattern in the shushing. It didn't sound like a heartbeat, but it sounded like something. *I'm here. I'm here. I'm here.*

CHAPTER SEVENTEEN

THERE WASN'T MUCH TO DO IN THE OLYMPIC VILLAGE. AT ST. Mary's, there was the daily—or, in Bristol's case, nightly—work to do to keep their little city running smoothly. Here, there was no work to do since the aid workers took total care of the cooking, the cleaning, the laundry. When they ran out of toiletries, aid workers brought them more. There was nothing to do apart from watching an old TV and playing games of foosball on a broken table. There were books, but not enough, and just browsing the selection was usually enough for most of them to wander over to the foosball table to watch a pair of people try to turn the stubby handles with their fingertips, lunging for the intact ones. On nights when his courage was up, Bristol drew outlines of the foosball players with pens on paper. Unlike in the USA, those materials never seemed to be in short supply.

They had been led to believe that Metrics, the United States government, had taken over the whole world, and that people in every geographic location on Earth lived as they lived. Since Metrics controlled what they saw, heard, and read on the news, there was no reason to believe otherwise. Bristol knew, for example, that the country he lived in had once been called the

United States, and the particular region where he lived had once been known as Pennsylvania, or something like that. He thought that these names were harmless tokens of moderate curiosity, but had long outworn their usefulness for describing meaningful aspects of a place, like laws and kinds of food and what the people looked like. As it turned out, the USA was still a place with its own culture—it had just been cut off from the rest of the world. Here, the people were still pale as paper. They ate meat, and lots of it, which was something they never did back home. Most of the refugees were constipated and miserable the first week, until the aid workers figured out that they shouldn't shock their digestive systems with multiple servings of dead pigs and sheep and cows every meal. Bristol found the idea of meat disgusting, but the taste delicious. After so many years living as an Unregistered citizen, he was used to switching the thinking, feeling part of his brain off, so he simply did that whenever he found meat on his plate. Here, only some people wore watches, and the ones who did didn't seem as interested in them as the people back home. Here, every night, the newscasters talked of liberating the United States.

It was a humanitarian crisis, they said. Millions of people had already been killed in the name of saving resources, and the way things were going, another wave of murders could be expected sometime in the next decade. By this, Bristol assumed they meant that eventually the resources would dwindle so that the Fours would eventually believe life would be better without the Fives, and so on. But every night, as they gathered around the dated television hanging on the wall to listen to the reports, a question nagged at him—what should he believe?

After all, for the better part of twenty years, he had believed whatever Metrics told him. The news didn't come on nightly; it was on twenty-four hours a day, with product placements instead of commercials so you never had a break from it, and everything they said had been a lie. What if this place was no different? What was he supposed to believe?

The information overload overwhelmed him and made him

tired, but it had a completely different effect on Samara. In the evenings, she was the first to claim a spot right in front of the TV. She talked to aid workers constantly about what was being done to liberate their home country. It confused Bristol to no end, having just found out that he *had* a home country. After just finding out that the help they were getting from Canada was just a small piece of the puzzle. After having to adjust his sleep schedule to fall asleep in the early night for the first time since he was a child. It was all just too much. All he wanted to do was sketch.

He also wanted Samara near, but couldn't stand it when she was either. When she was physically around him, all that talk of home made him sick. Worse, she'd started to talk about subjects he barely understood, and he didn't want to risk looking stupid by asking for the basics. What, for example, was the United Countries? Was it what they'd been told, a world government, but a different one from Metrics? Sometimes it sounded like it was an army. He'd never heard of it before, obviously, and he didn't know how Samara was keeping up at such a pace.

One night, about a week after they'd arrived, he asked to walk Samara to her room.

"Sure," she said.

Samara stopped early on to say hi to Taye, and the two of them chatted about what they'd just heard from the newscasters for a while. Bristol crossed his arms and leaned against the wall to watch foosball while he waited for their conversation to end. When it finally did, Bristol worried that his courage wouldn't hold.

"Mind if I come in for a minute?" he asked when they got to her door.

She looked at him quizzically. "Can you?"

"I think so."

Samara smiled and scrunched her eyes. "It's hard to get used to this life with no rules. Of course."

They went inside. His heart pounded against his ribs while he watched her take off her shoes. Ugly white tennis shoes that someone else had been walking around in before she'd decided that they were good enough for a refugee but not for her. Watching Samara with them hurt—the way she untied each with her long fingers instead of just kicking them off. She took care of her things, and she deserved better things to take care of.

She looked up at him. "Are you okay?"

He reached out and drew her close to him until their ribs were touching and he could feel her heart beating. "No," he said into her hair. "I miss you." That wasn't the way he'd rehearsed this.

She pulled her face away to look at him and rest her hands on his shoulders. "I'm right here."

"I just miss being close to you. I've been thinking..."

"Yes?"

"I've been thinking about Denver and Stephen. All week I've been hearing the baby's heartbeat in my dreams, when I dream..."

She closed her eyes under a tense brow. "Bristol, stop."

"We'd be great at it, you and me."

She turned her face away. "Stop."

"If we got married, we could stay in the same room and then I could take care of you and—"

"Take care of *me*? Who's going to take care of you? I don't know if you noticed, but we're not exactly in a place to take care of anyone right now. We're being kept, held, until more rich and powerful people decide what to do with us. This isn't the time to think about marriage and babies, Bristol."

He was glad he'd prepared for a fight. "Why not? I think this is the perfect time—we need each other now more than ever. And why would we wait for someone else to decide what our lives are worth? We tried that, both on the outside—"

"In the United States," Samara cut in, using the new, strange name for home.

"Yes, both there and at St. Mary's. And now we're here and we get another chance at living our own lives, no matter what is going on around us." He grasped both of her hands in his. "Marry me.

Bring a baby here with me. You're right—life with no rules is hard to get used to, but we'll never get used to it if we don't try."

She kept his hands in hers and knocked her forehead against his chest. "I can't."

Bristol paused. "Is it something else?"

"What do you mean?"

"You know what I mean."

"I truly don't."

"Some*one* else?"

Samara sighed. "It's so many things, Bristol. I wasn't prepared for this conversation tonight. You and I haven't even really talked about this since..."

"July seventh."

"Right. It's been so long and we've been through so much that I haven't had time to think things through. I'm not saying it's not someone else, I'm just saying that if it is, they're just a small part of the big picture."

Now Bristol closed his eyes and listened to his breath. A rising anger burned in his stomach as he recalled the sight of Taye carrying Samara out of the meeting house. Taye going with Samara at lunch. Taye and Samara chatting about the news...

"If that's true," said Bristol, "will you promise me to think about it?"

"I don't think it's a good idea, Bristol."

He waved his hand to dispel his silly dream. "Forget getting married. Forget the baby. Just promise me to think about what you want. *Who* you want."

She bit her lip. "Okay."

"That means you'll have to give up some of your news obsession."

"That's not fair." Her voice was suddenly dark. "I didn't ask you for a proposal."

"Well, let me know when you sort out your feelings and you won't get another one."

"Fine." She opened the door and stepped aside.

Bristol nodded to her and stepped out, fighting every instinct he had to hold her, breathe in the scent of her hair, tell her he was sorry. The door closed behind him before he was more than a step away.

CHAPTER EIGHTEEN

SAMARA DIDN'T SEE BRISTOL THE NEXT MORNING AT BREAKFAST, nor at lunch. She was beginning to worry about him. Just because she didn't want to add giving birth to her to-do list didn't mean she didn't care. She knew what Bristol was capable of, the thoughts he was capable of turning into unnerving images. The vivid beauty of his mind. She could even see his point, though she hesitated to admit it. They could be great together, and it wasn't fair that there always seemed to be someone around to tell them no.

But Samara was hungry, and insatiably so, not for food (there was, for once in her life, more than enough to eat every meal) but for knowledge. Bristol had a point there, too; he'd named it as her obsession. She was even a little afraid of it and noticed how willingly she'd connect the dots on bizarre theories that couldn't possibly be true. The campers—or the Unregistered, or the refugees, or whatever people with more power were calling them now—had begun to make up their own stories of where they were and what fates awaited them, each theory as unlikely as the last. In her intense craving for information, Samara found herself wanting to pick a few to believe.

She talked to the aid workers as much as she could, but they weren't much use. She recognized the type: do-gooders who didn't have an ounce more intelligence than she did herself. She saw herself in them, and she loathed herself for it. She'd wasted too much of her life following protocol, not asking questions. Now that she wanted to know, there was nowhere to turn. Her watch was probably in a police department somewhere. Not, she reminded herself, that it would be much good anyway. The search network they'd always used to get answers was controlled by Metrics and provided the public with mostly false information.

Though it was freezing outside, she put on her new-to-her coat and hat and headed outside for a walk. The streets of Edinburgh never ceased to cheer her, though there was always a short period where she had to adjust to being one of few brown people on the street. It didn't bother her too much, just when she saw people staring at her. She usually noticed it only at the very beginning of her walk, then had the rest of her afternoon to just enjoy the winding streets and the colorful shop windows.

She was just passing a small tea room and getting into one of her favorite daydreams—that she'd one day have money to buy a cup of tea and sit to drink it there—when someone waved to her from the window. She stopped and recognized the friendly face. What was Taye doing inside a tea room?

A bell tinkled softly from far above Samara's head when she opened the door. The room warmed her chapped cheeks and she inhaled the spicy scent of something baked and sweet. Taye had been seated at a table near the window, but he stood when she walked in and gestured to her. Samara looked around, suddenly aware of how her skin and clothes separated her from the other patrons, painfully aware that she didn't have any money to buy anything.

Surprisingly, Taye had a cup of half-finished tea on his table, as well as an empty plate littered with crumbs. He stepped toward the empty chair and held it out for Samara. "On your walk already? You usually pass here much later."

She wouldn't ask how he knew—that's what he wanted and she could tell. "I decided to make the loop backward today."

"I see you every day. I usually sit there by the other window, but there was a family there today."

"What are you doing here?"

"What do you mean? I'm having a cup of tea. I'm people-watching."

"How did you buy that?" Her eyes pointed to the cup. "You don't have a watch anymore, and I'm not even sure they use those for transactions here."

"They don't. Well, some of them do, but it's not common yet." He ran a hand through his wavy hair, like a movie star on a break from filming but still in costume. "I just walked in and asked if I could have it."

Samara paused. "You walked in..."

"...and I asked if they could spare a cup of tea and a biscuit. And whadoyaknow, they could."

"Did you tell them you were a refugee?"

Taye snorted and briefly glanced around at the other tables. "I didn't have to. We don't exactly have a typical Scottish look, do we?"

"You come in every day, and they just give you free food?"

"Yep. Every day for the past four days, anyway. They seem happy to give it. I can get some for you, too. Are you hungry?" He flashed a smile.

It had been so long since she'd eaten something purely for pleasure. There was plenty of food at Olympic Village, but no decadence. She'd never tasted chocolate before, but she'd seen it in display cases and store windows, and she recognized crumbs of it on Taye's plate. Her mouth watered just thinking about what it must be like. Only Threes and above were allowed to buy it back home. Taye saw her looking and grinned. He made a motion to the short, stout woman behind the counter and pointed to Samara. In no time, two small saucers appeared at her elbow; one with a cup full of steaming tea, and the other with a thin wafer covered in chocolate. She thanked the little woman and stared at the gifts.

"This doesn't feel exactly right," she said.

"That's because you haven't tasted the biscuit yet. The best way is to dip it into the tea, just for a second."

Samara picked up the biscuit like a forbidden fruit, taking in the smooth, cool surface. Then she dunked it into her tea and took a bite. It was everything she wanted—sweet and warm and irresistibly indulgent. She let her eyelids meet.

"I'm glad you came in," said Taye. "I usually wave at you, but you don't see me. You always look a little..."

"What?"

He looked out the window, then leaned across the table to focus his eyes on hers. "Lost in thought. You had that look today, too. I thought you were going to pass by again."

The little woman from behind the counter was back now, this time with a miniature legal pad and a pen. "Hello, I'm Anna-Margaret." She poised her pen. "What's your name, please?"

Samara looked from Taye to Anna-Margaret. "Hello, Anna-Margaret. I'm Samara."

"Some-ah-rah?" She gave the notepad a flabbergasted smile. "That's quite...unique! How do you spell that?"

"I'm sorry, Anna-Margaret. I promise I'll come back in as soon as I can to pay you back for this." Samara felt the heat of shame on her face as she glanced down at the half-eaten biscuit.

"Oh? Oh—I'm not writing an IOU!" Anna-Margaret did a funny sort of laugh that sounded like she found Samara's comment more sad than humorous.

Taye leaned in again. "She's writing our stories."

"Gonna put out a book about all of you." Anna-Margaret nodded. "Taye tells me you've got a very interesting one, about watching a boy saw off his own hand. Just titillating! Tell me all about it."

A memory flashed without warning and she was suddenly there again, in the prison kitchen, watching the guards open a cupboard to discover Jude's little hand inside. What he'd gone through, how he'd made the choice so quickly, she'd never understand. It wasn't her story to tell. And it certainly wasn't Anna-Margaret's. The sweet smell was suddenly making Samara sick.

"Excuse me," she said and pressed her hands into the table to support herself as she stood. Anna-Margaret and Taye seemed to be talking about her, but all she cared about was feeling the familiar sting of cold on her face.

Seconds after she left, she heard the bell's jingle follow someone else out.

"Hey!" Taye called. "Wait up."

Samara turned around. "How could you sell our stories? Jude's story?"

"I...I didn't think it was a big deal!" He looked more sheepish than she'd ever seen him. "She's just a nice lady who doesn't have anything exciting in her life, so she wants—"

"She wants fifteen minutes of fame."

"No—what?"

"She's writing a book."

"So?"

"So people read books here." Samara pointed down the street. "There's a whole shop in this city that sells nothing but books, and people buy them."

Taye's mouth curled. "No, they don't."

"Yes, they do. Some people even get famous for writing books. They get their pictures on the covers!"

Taye threw his hands on top of his head and snickered. "I'll believe it when I see it."

"Then see it. Come on." Samara walked with heated purpose toward her favorite spot in Edinburgh. Taye, with his longer legs, easily kept up, though Samara became slightly winded from walking so quickly.

Finally, it was in sight—a large blue building with black trim and wide windows displaying stacks of real, paper books, some as thick as her fist. In the United States, there were still a few flimsy notebooks around for people in real need of technology or in specialized professions, but hardly any books. There had been no need for books, because people did not read them. Samara had always been told that it was a waste of time—that people in the past didn't get as much done in their daily lives because they had to sit and read to learn something. If she and her friends wanted to learn something, they'd do a quick search on their watches, speedily scan an article for relevant information, and be on their way.

That was the world Taye was used to, too. Now he stared at the window, mouth open, in dumbstruck silence. Together, they watched an old man with a balding scalp and thick-rimmed glasses approach the counter with several books in his arms. He paid and left, nodding to them both as he hurried away.

"It's called a book shop. And people really read them. I've seen them." She hugged her jacket a little more snugly to her chest. "But I think they do it for different reasons. Some really want to learn, to connect. And others just want a little excitement in their lives. That's what you'd be selling for chocolate biscuits."

"I didn't know."

"Well, now you do. For the record, it's fine with me if that's the price for your stories. It's none of my business. But don't give them mine, or anyone else's."

She walked away. After a few paces she allowed herself a look back and saw that Taye had walked inside the book shop. She smiled in spite of herself. Taye, charming and shameless, would probably return in a few hours with a bag full of free books. And she'd probably approach him after the news that evening to ask what he'd seen in there. But for now, she was exhausted by two arguments in less than twenty-four hours and let her mind rest while she walked, hoping, as always, to get herself lost.

CHAPTER NINETEEN

FOR THE FIRST TIME IN HIS LIFE, JUDE COULD READ FACES. AND he realized he'd been able to do it for a while now. It was like he'd been wearing sunglasses and had lost the lenses. The world was suddenly brighter and more colorful, but he wasn't sure when it had happened because he was still wearing the frames.

He scanned the room for Samara as his fellow refugees shuffled in, claiming their spots on the sofa, on the floor, leaning against walls, all facing the small television hanging from the ceiling. He kept his eyes focused on the doorway, aware of the pull of the TV, but stubbornly refusing to give it his attention just yet. All those food commercials only made him hungry and dissatisfied with the meals they were given here.

Cork came bouncing in, a friendly recognition in his face.

"What's up, Reeder?" he asked as he took Samara's spot next to him on the sofa.

"Nothing." He smiled back at him and gave him the now-customary little jab on his arm before Cork could do it first. "Have you seen Miss Shepherd?"

"Nope."

This was another nice element about the TV; no longer did Jude have to awkwardly wait for conversations to end or think of something to say next. The mysterious allure of the current commercial had already pulled Cork in, abruptly ending the exchange. It was both similar and vastly different from the communication problems people had about their watches. Back in America, where everyone wore them, conversations were still common, but much slower. Someone would start to say something, then look at their watch to make sure their assertion was correct, then the second person would check too, and the rest of the conversation would be piecemeal, dragging on word by word until both were so absorbed in whatever they were looking at that it wasn't crucial to continue talking anymore. Jude would often be the first to look at his watch in an attempt to get out of talking, if someone started a conversation with him at all. The only exception was his parents—they were always on their watches so much that it wasn't even worth saying hello.

Jude could also tell something was wrong with Samara as soon as she entered the room. He got up, nodding to an older woman to indicate she could have his spot on the sofa.

Samara's lips were badly chapped from her walk, and she bit the lower one as Jude approach her. "I'm sorry," said Jude. "I tried to save your spot, but—"

"It's okay, Jude. I'm not mad at you."

Jude considered her a moment. *It figures,* he thought. *Just when I thought I could see feelings.*

"I'm mad," she continued, "at our situation."

"Mad at our situation?"

"I'm mad that they tell us lies or nothing at all. I'm mad that we're not in charge of our futures. I'm mad that our grandparents traded our freedom for convenience, mad that they couldn't wake up long enough to make sure our lives were as independent as theirs had been."

Jude hated when adults talked like this, but Samara wasn't a real adult. She was only seven years older than he was. Still, he didn't like to think of himself as this scared and helpless seven years from now. He crept closer to her, cupped his hands around her ear and whispered, "The Red Sea is still alive."

Samara closed her eyes. "I hear that too, Jude, almost every day. That's another thing I'm mad about—I can't believe how much lack of real information makes me willing to believe these crazy theories. There is no Red Sea anymore. Metrics destroyed the safe houses; they destroyed the people in them. We're all that's left."

Jude shook his head and kept his gaze on his teacher's face. "I need to show you something outside."

"Outside? Can it wait until after the broadcast?"

Jude shook his head. "I think it's better to do it during the news, since everyone will be in here and they won't see us leave."

Samara groaned and touched a fingertip to her lips.

What he needed to show her was only two blocks from Olympic Village, but it took them longer to walk than he thought —Samara lagged behind him. Still, what Jude needed to show her was something he couldn't quite put into words, so he slowed his pace to match hers. Finally, they came to a small courtyard between two buildings. It was well-kept and manicured, and when he'd first seen it earlier that day, he'd taken it for a rich person's mini-oasis amid the busy city life. Now, it was dark and there were no lights on, so the pristine grass and lush flowers were all shaded in dark. The only light came from the streetlights, which flooded the streets and overflowed just slightly into the courtyard. It wasn't much, but it was enough to see what they'd come for.

Jude stopped in the very center of the garden, where a circle of stones enclosed some ashes. He pointed at the ground and looked at Samara. Samara studied it for a moment, and turned back to Jude. "What is this? It looks like a fire pit. Sometimes, people light fires for fun—"

"This wasn't like that. Look closer," Jude said. "See that stalk? Earlier today, this was a bush."

"Someone set it on fire?"

Jude nodded. A burning bush—he'd never seen a real one, but the phrase alone was code within the Red Sea. To see a burning bush was to inform others that help was near.

The door to one of the buildings lining the garden creaked open, but the face behind it was hidden in the darkness. "Psst."

Jude caught his breath in his upper chest, but Samara took his hand and squeezed it. "We can't see you," she said to the crack.

Instead of opening the door further, a hand snaked out of the opening and beckoned them inside. Jude looked again at the ashy stump and tugged at Samara's hand. They walked together toward the door.

Whoever had been at the door was gone now, and the door was just slightly ajar. Samara made a motion to walk in front of Jude to enter first, but Jude quickly moved so he'd be the first to go in. No sense losing one of their best minds for his mistake—she'd have time to run if things went wrong. They followed a narrow, dimly-lit corridor to another door, this one formidable, standing tall and thick with ornate flowers carved into the unpainted wood. As Jude reached for the brass knob, it turned on its own.

A tall man in shirtsleeves and suspenders opened it, gave them a short appraising look, then smiled and opened the door wider. Jude let out a barking laugh to see who was sitting there.

Bristol, Denver, Stephen, Taye, Nurse Sue, Karale, and Danovan were all seated in a mishmash of beautifully upholstered chairs and sofas among several other people whom Jude didn't know. Although there was no fire in the fireplace, the low lights on the tables cast their faces in a stunning glow. The people Jude knew from the monastery suddenly appeared much different from how Jude remembered them; they were clean and on their way to being healthy, and they smiled beautifully and gave exclamations of welcome to see Jude and Samara.

Bristol laughed and looked only at Jude. "The dream team," he said.

"What's this?" asked Jude.

The man in shirtsleeves picked up a glass of amber liquid from one of the side tables. "This is the Red Sea." He brought the glass to his lips and took a surprisingly dainty sip for a man of his size. "Edinburgh chapter."

CHAPTER TWENTY

"Of course, the relocation badly damaged the Red Sea in America."

"In America?" asked Samara. "Why would you need it anywhere else?"

"Technically, the Red Sea is an international aid group." The man was the only individual in the room whom Samara didn't recognize. He spoke with an accent, but Samara's ears seemed to mold around the words easier. Maybe she was getting used to the new sounds. "We give money to countries in need."

"Wouldn't the government get that money, then?" she asked.

"Not necessarily," said the man, who, now that Samara had a closer view of him, had visible tattoos running out from his sleeves onto his arms, hands, and fingers. More tattoos sprang up from his neck to the base of his skull. She could only guess at the multitude he had hidden under his shirt. "If we think the government is oppressing the people, the money goes to the rebels. There was a big rebel network in America, but they didn't have a name for themselves. So they just started calling themselves after their benefactors."

"Is the Red Sea still giving money to the rebels in America?"

The man looked at her, surprised. "Sadly, no. Don't you know?"

"Know what?"

Kareale drew herself up tall. "We were the last undiscovered camp. Say what you want about our leadership, but we kept you alive."

Danovan closed his eyes. "Please."

The man in the shirtsleeves just smiled wide. "Why not? Whatever happened when you were there, it's over now. And you lived to see the other side!"

Kareale's chunky sweater sagged from her shoulders and her collarbone could be seen from just above the neckline, but still she pressed her lips together as if willing herself to feel pride in what she had done. Samara considered her. Just a few weeks ago, she would have balked at the idea of calling her an effective leader. But they had all survived; was it luck, or did Samara and the others have Karaele, Danovan, and Tommy to thank? Was there truly a way of keeping people both free and safe?

"My name is Daniel," the man said, crossing one colorful arm over the other. "I work for the Red Sea."

Samara might have been in another country, but she recognized a fellow Five when she saw one. Whatever his role in this organization, he couldn't be very high up.

Denver, frowning, seemed to have the same idea. "What exactly do you do, Daniel?"

"Education. I give workshops at schools and talk to groups of people who are interested in our cause. We have programs in fourteen different countries, but the work we did in America was considered the most important."

Denver snorted. "So it was the biggest failure."

"That's one way of saying it. But there are much bigger fish to fry here. I called you all together to inform you of what you won't hear on the news."

Samara sat up straighter, angling herself slightly away from Bristol.

"You've probably heard on the news that the rest of the world is pretty worried about America and your government. Apparently, Metrics is so worried about word getting out that they're not actually a worldwide government that they're making plans to make it a reality."

Jude scrunched his nose. "You mean they actually want to take over the world?"

"No, they could never do that. They've been depleting their own resources for years. But they still have some weapons. They completely closed their borders, but they refused to give those up."

Stephen's face went white. "They want to attack? Here?"

"Probably somewhere in the UK. They know that we provided resources to their rebels, and we think they caught wind of our plan to infiltrate their citizen's watches with information. We were successful at that, but Metrics managed to convince most of them that it was a hoax."

"What about the ones who believed?"

"If they showed any indication of real belief, you can guess where they are now."

Samara imagined the prisons, emptied since the relocation, with new inmates trickling in. What did prisons look like now, with no Unregistered workers? At least the guards had something to do now.

"Why haven't they done it yet?"

"Because our weapons are superior, and your leaders know it. Your President is afraid we'd retaliate."

Most of the room spoke at once. "President?" They looked around, and a cheerless chuckle passed through the room.

"Yes, America still has a President."

"They just told us that the Ones ran everything."

"The Ones *do* run everything." Daniel's eyes sparkled with a secret. "Has anyone ever met a One?"

"Of course not. They're the leaders; you wouldn't just bump into one of them on the street—"

"That's because the only Ones are the President and his family.

Your President's grandfather was in power for almost twenty years, and then when he died, they organized the Tier system to keep themselves in total control."

"No," said Samara, the teacher in her rising to the occasion. "There was an uprising of citizens. They demanded a Tier system—"

"That's the story they told you, yes." said Daniel gently.

Samara spoke slowly, the words coming into her own mind as she spoke them aloud: "I always thought they were just another Tier. Just like us, but richer and bred for leadership."

"Definitely richer. That family owns most of the private business in America. Bred for leadership? What kind of leader isolates their own country and forbids citizens from forming bonds with each other? What kind of leader encourages its people to spy on each other and report each other from a young age?"

"The kind of leaders who murder their own people," said Bristol with his eyes set to the quiet fireplace. "We know what it's like there, even if we haven't been privy to the inner workings. You don't have to get us outraged."

"My brother is right," said Denver. "So, Daniel, you've called together the refugees who are interested enough in the Red Sea to notice the signal. We appreciate your information, but..."

"But what do you want?" Bristol finished for her.

"I'm an organizer." Daniel threw his head back, and with it, his drink. "I want to get you organized."

Samara perceived a subtle change in the room as all noises, most nearly inaudible anyway, stopped completely. Ice seemed to cease floating inside glasses, chairs no longer creaked with weight shifts. The only sound that could be heard, apart from the whistling wind at the windows, was Daniel's glass hitting the deep ebony side table.

"The Red Sea thinks the rebel cause in America is done. Since our government rescued you, there's no one left there to fund. But the Red Sea has still been doing some hefty lifting for you all."

"Hefty lifting?" Bristol's tone was hesitant.

"I only know this because I heard my boss speaking to his boss. Under the threat of war, our government is considering a trade."

The weight of his words hit Samara hard in the stomach. "Us for a promise of peace."

"Yes. Only some members of Parliament, though. The dangerous ones who aren't good for the UK anyway. The Red Sea is trying to convince them that you're valuable enough to keep."

"It'll never happen." Stephen leaned his back against his plush chair, as if trying a little too hard to radiate calm. "Don't the people choose their leaders here? Considering the reception we received, I'd say we're pretty popular. The aid workers tell us it's a matter of national pride that we were brought here."

"It is," said Daniel. "But you're not as popular as you think—at least not with everyone. There are some people in our country who would like to have a light version of what you had back in America."

"Metrics?" asked Jude, slack-jawed. "They *want* a government like Metrics?"

"Oddly enough, yeah, they do. They just haven't thought things through yet. But they'd rather Scotland be isolated, they'd rather not have to deal with little inconveniences like finding a mate, and they'd be told explicitly that they're better than other people."

"They don't understand," said Jude.

"You're right; they don't. But you can't force someone to care about other people; you can't make someone love people."

Danovan cleared his throat. "But these people—these policy-makers and the people that elect them—they're only doing it to protect themselves, right? Sometimes you have to do terrible things for the greater good."

"You would know," said Denver, her features tight.

"Don't get started. I'm saying these people are just trying to protect their families and friends, people they care about. Nothing wrong with that, but we've got to protect ours. Maybe we should plan on..."

"What?" asked Stephen, taking Denver's hand. It was gesture

that was more than a loving token—Samara suspected it was to stop Denver from jumping up and slapping Danovan herself. "Assassinating the members of Parliament who pose a threat to us?"

"Yes, as a matter of fact, that *is* what I was thinking!"

Bristol stood. "It takes no courage to care for the people you know. Look at the mess America is in. Look at President Whatever-his-name-is. Even *he* protected his family. It takes guts to sacrifice for someone you *don't* know, to have faith that people are worth saving even if you don't know anything about them. Even if you don't like the things you *do* know about them." Danovan's spine slumped forward as he swirled his drink around in his glass. Bristol seemed surprised to have shut him up but unsure of how long he'd stay silent. "So, yes, we need to do something about these people in Scotland who don't want us here, and we need to address the underlying fear. But we can't heal the fear of killing by killing."

Samara leaned back into her chair and crossed her arms. *Damnit, Bristol.* Would she ever be able to truly fall out of love with him? The answer was there for the taking, but she pushed it away and turned back to Daniel. "I assume you were thinking diplomacy?"

"Well, yes." Daniel's eyes still showed a little surprise; maybe he hadn't guessed that such placid-looking refugees would possibly discuss assassinating members of his Parliament in his house. "But in the spirit of democracy, I think we should take a vote."

Diplomacy was unanimous; Danovan and Kareale abstained, both looking toward the ground as the others raised their hands in support of a peaceful strategy.

What to do next proved more troublesome. Committees were organized to drum up public support and to do more research on the leaders who posed a risk.

"Obviously, Bristol should be on the public support committee," said Samara to Jude, who'd found a paper and pen. "But I want to be on the research committee."

Bristol took in a long breath and let out a longer one. "But," said Samara, "I'd like to help with you, too, Bristol. I know someone who wants our stories. She's writing a book."

CHAPTER TWENTY-ONE

DENVER'S CHIN FELT HEAVY IN HER HAND. SHE SAT FOR A LONG time at the table after dinner, trying to summon the strength to get up and walk to Nurse Sue's room. Maybe she'd just wait a little longer. Maybe then the nurse would come downstairs herself to watch the nightly news with everyone.

Denver's waistline wasn't the only piece of her growing thicker. Her thoughts, once quick and limber, seemed to move slower, as if her brain were running in water. Being among civilized society made her think of her old life, of energy shots and fast-paced games on her watch, of deadlines and of her lighting-round sessions on the treadmill. Here, life was slower, and so was she. She wasn't exactly sure what was causing this gradual weakening, but there was plenty to blame: the cold weather, the monotony of Olympic Village, the heavy meals, the baby. She was still in a bit of denial that there was actually a human inside her.

She felt most connected to him—she had a feeling it was a boy —when she was in the bathtub, which was almost every night. Stephen, perhaps trying to be useful, would draw a bath for her and drape a towel and her clean clothes over the door. He always said he wished he had something else to give her besides the plain white bar of soap and bottle of thick white shampoo. Once she asked him what he meant, exactly, and he mentioned the sweeter-smelling soaps back in America. Just a few months ago, back when she was a Three with plenty of money to burn, her baths were infused with peppermint bath bombs, crushed lavender blossoms, candles. She would have turned her nose up at those terribly gooey soaps with the artificial scents and looked down on Stephen for suggesting them. Now, though, knowing he wanted to give them to her was touching, even to her. Still, she only wanted to be emotionally touched by Stephen—once, when he tried to climb into the tub with her, she stretched her legs out and told him it was too cramped for the two of them. He left her alone in the bathroom, looking more than a little disappointed, but it was for his own good. Denver ran hand over her belly again and remembered the sound of the wand from her first doctor's appointment. *I'm here, I'm here, I'm here.*

Denver knew she was not doing her share of work for the Red Sea, and though she knew it was important, she was tired. She didn't quite know how Samara was doing it; since their meeting at Daniel's house, she never seemed to sleep. Sleep was all Denver wanted to do. While most of the rest of the refugees were busy going out and engaging, researching, and strategizing, Denver was napping and trying not to throw up her lunch.

Nurse Sue did eventually come down the steps. When she saw Denver, she came over to make a fuss over her belly.

"How are you feeling?"

"Exhausted," answered Denver.

"It's normal," Nurse Sue said. "Your body is building the placenta right now. You'll feel tired even if you're not doing anything."

"I'm never doing anything," Denver said. "I can't afford to be this tired right now. You know what's at stake."

"There are two hundred people here. Only one of us has a baby to take care of. You're allowed to focus on that little one. How is Stephen?"

"He's fine."

"Maybe he could help you out. Give you a back rub."

"You don't know my husband. Since we lost our focus injections, everything makes Stephen want to..."

"Make love?"

Denver felt the burn on her face creep up to her eyebrows. "Yes, in fact. Yes. Obviously that would be a disaster."

Nurse Sue looked perplexed. "What?"

"That's how we got into this situation." Denver laid her hand just under her belly button, where she perceived the baby to be. "Can you imagine if we created another little—"

"Denver!" Nurse Sue laughed and slapped both of her knees. "You can make love to your husband! You won't get pregnant again. Even if you have sex every day until the baby's born, your belly has a single-occupancy maximum."

Denver felt herself coil inward, then immediately rise to her own defense. "How was I supposed to know that? No one ever told me that."

"I'm sorry, dear. They would have told you in your pregnancy classes if you'd conceived under the Metrics rules."

"It won't hurt the baby?"

There was a kindness to Nurse Sue's face that made Denver think of her mother, far away and without either of her children. Denver's sense of motherhood was so small, yet when she thought of her mom all alone and unsure of whether her children were living or dead, she felt a chasm in her heart and knew her mom wouldn't be whole again until she saw them. They had to survive. Somehow, Denver would tell her mother someday that she had a grandchild. She needed to look forward to that.

"The baby won't notice a thing. It's quite safe. And I think," said Nurse Sue, "it might benefit both of you."

She was probably right. Since the Red Sea meeting, Stephen had been working himself past exhaustion with the rest of the assembly. That evening, he drew her bath again. She took her time with her baby, dried off, and, not touching the clothes he'd draped over the door for her, slipped into bed beside him.

She didn't expect his reaction. "What are you doing?" he asked.

"I just...wanted to be close to you."

"Oh." He inched slightly toward her, newspaper still in hand, not moving the little notebook that lay between them. She glanced down at it, catching a few words in his messy handwriting. *European Convention of Human Rights...violation...*he'd underlined it three times.

"I'll get that out of your way," Stephen said, grabbing the notebook.

"Thanks," she said softly, scooted closer, and kissed his shoulder. "I was talking to Nurse Sue today."

He looked up from his paper, the news still in his eyes as he looked at her. "Is the baby okay?"

"Yes. I told her that I was afraid of getting pregnant again or hurting him if we had sex again."

Stephen looked horrified. "I didn't even think of that! It's a good thing we stopped—"

"She says it's safe. We can...if you want to."

He flung the newspaper, notebook, and pen onto the floor and dove at her. "I want to. I want to." He said those words over and over, until, under Denver's laugh, they sounded like *I want you, I want you.*

CHAPTER TWENTY-TWO

BACK HOME, IF BRISTOL WANTED TO PAINT, HE HAD TO SNEAK out in the middle of the night with an ice pack under his glove to disable his tracking chip and hide from street cameras long enough to stencil a simple design on a wall. Here, it turned out that it was as easy as asking someone's permission.

He'd gone with Samara to the little teahouse to tell his tale of escape. When Samara told the woman writing down Bristol's story that he was a street artist, she became excited and called for her boss. The owner of the teahouse turned out to be a woman with a collected sort of quality about her. She was thin, but not the same kind of thin they were. Beneath her red cardigan, Bristol pictured toned biceps from her sessions with a personal trainer. Denver used to go to sessions like that.

"He's a street artist." Anna-Margaret pointed at Bristol. "He used to paint political pictures on walls. *Illegal* pictures. These two say it drove those Metrics lads mad."

The owner of the teahouse arranged her arms in front of her, but drew a polished nail at the edge of her lip. She glanced down at Anna-Margaret's pen and paper. "Can you show me?"

"Draw the nun," Samara said. What was there in her voice?

Was it pride? Nostalgia? Bristol was still defenseless against her, and though his fingers still felt stiff and he knew before he started that it wouldn't come out exactly right, he sketched the nun as he remembered her on the wall in front of Samara's window back home.

While he drew, Samara cleared her throat and addressed the teahouse owner. "Bristol played a big role in sparking hope among us. He helped people escape."

"Escape?"

"Yes, literally and metaphorically. We're American refugees, in case you didn't know." If she did know, she didn't indicate it. She only kept gazing down at the paper and the blood now dripping—though pathetically imperfectly—from the nun's hand. "Now we're concerned that Parliament wants to send us back."

"Wouldn't that be...illegal?"

"Frowned upon, but not illegal," Samara said confidently. "We've been doing research on refugee rights, and they're surprisingly sparse. The best we can hope for is public support."

Bristol's drawing was far from finished, but he sensed this was the right time to show her. With two fingers, he slid the illustration across the table. The lighting in here was good for it; the large windows let in the light from the overcast sky. The woman picked up the drawing and examined it for a few seconds. "I'll have to inform our landlord. Can you start tomorrow?"

———

The morning after his tearoom mural was featured in the local newspaper accompanied by Bristol's story (Samara had asked to be kept out of it), four more businesses in the area called the Olympic Village requesting he recreate his old protest images on their buildings, too. Bristol felt a burst of new energy in his blood, sparkling wildly, as he searched his mind and sketched.

Mornings were usually for too much coffee and short walks around the building, but now he felt he had a purpose again, that he could do more than simply wait for his life to begin. He started to see these images in a new light as he drew them from his memory. Whatever they had done for other people, it came nowhere close to what they had done for *him*. While most of the other Unregistered he knew used too much drift and abused most people in their lives, including themselves, with a rage they didn't fully understand, Bristol had learned to live as an Unregistered. Not just survive, but to live without resentment and with genuine love for his sister and mother. Because of this obsession with getting these pictures out on a page—or on a wall—Bristol had access to love.

He turned the paper over and let his hands do the work without his mind in the way. Soon, there was another image on his paper: a man with a bony boy frame, facing away and brandishing a can of spray paint. The back of his hat didn't hide his short neck. Bristol colored in the skin on his arms thickly with his pencil. Out of the can, a line of hearts spewed onto the page.

"What's that?"

Bristol's hand instinctively went to cover what he'd done, as he had for too many years trying to hide his work from Denver. He'd show her, eventually, when he was done, but she was never satisfied. When he realized it was Samara who was standing behind him, though, he inched the drawing closer to her.

"I realized this is what's been missing from my life. I thought I was lost because of all the changes—you know, the old camp, and this new camp. But it wasn't that. It was because I'd gotten away from this."

"You've gotten away from your real love," she said.

It struck Bristol as an odd choice of words, so he hesitated before he agreed.

"I'm really glad to hear that, Bristol, especially after the last time we talked. I've been feeling bad about what I said."

Bristol leapt to his feet. "Do you mean you've thought about my question?"

"Not...thoroughly. But I'm trying." She was speaking much

faster than she usually did. "That's not what I came over here to say."

From across the room, Taye flicked his yellow scarf over his shoulder and leaned into the door to open it to the outside. Now that he was standing beside her, Bristol noticed that Samara, too, was dressed for an outdoor walk. He seethed.

"I came over here to tell you that I just got off the phone with the Scottish Museum of Contemporary Art. They want to talk to you. Can you meet with them this morning?"

"I have to finish these. I'm supposed to start on a wall tomorrow downtown—"

"It won't take long. I think this could be really good for the cause."

Bristol looked at her and sighed. Why did he find it so hard to say no to her when she found it so easy to say it to him?

"Okay."

She brightened. "Great! Get your coat and I'll meet you by the front doors."

"You're coming with me?"

She grinned, hooking her thumbs inside the furry collar of her coat. "Where'd you think I was going?"

CHAPTER TWENTY-THREE

JUDE LIFTED HIS FEET AND EXAMINED HIS NEW SNEAKERS. Trainers, the aid worker had called them, but he was pretty sure she meant sneakers. They were the kind that might have gotten him bullied at his old school—bright red with yellow stripes—but that was a long time ago. Besides, it wasn't like he had a choice. They took what was donated. JoJo, sitting beside Jude and still wearing the shoes they'd given him upon arrival—white canvas slip-ons a size or two too big—looked at him with his mouth open in an awe-tinged smile.

"Now you can play football!" said JoJo.

Jude wanted to tell him how much he hated sports, but instead he said, "Yeah. Maybe. Cork and I are going to go for a walk first, though."

"Can I come?"

JoJo was making more requests like this every day. Jude knew the cool thing to do would be to blow him off, like Cork did with Henry. *Henry!* Jude could hear him saying. *Get out of here. We're not playing; we're doing work for the Red Sea!* But Jude couldn't say those things to JoJo. He liked having JoJo as his roommate; he liked when he followed him around the Olympic Village. It was almost like having a little brother, but better because Jude's parents weren't around. He wouldn't want any little brother of his going through the same experiences he'd been through with them; the meetings with the teachers and the doctor's appointments and the disappointed, downcast looks. Always talking to someone else, never to him. *Why isn't he living up to his genetic potential?*

Actually, Jude and Cork had official business to attend to, but he knew if he revealed this to JoJo, it would just strengthen his pleas. "Not right now," he said. "But later this afternoon, we can go to the park together."

JoJo smiled with every one of his teeth.

Jude met Cork at the front door and the two of them once again headed for the house with the burnt stump in the courtyard and did the rhythmic knock on the door. Daniel answered at once.

"Ready?" he asked the boys with a smile. "I've got some tea here for us."

They stepped inside and they began their daily briefing; which leaders were facing pressure from which sides, what did public opinion polls show about attitudes toward refugees. What Jude was most interested in hearing about was what the United States was doing, but since they had closed their borders and installed tighter security on their technology, they really only knew what Metrics released. That information was, as Daniel put it, "As worthless as tits on a nun." Jude didn't know what tits were, but he knew about nuns from the night he was arrested, and realized he was supposed to laugh at this. He laughed.

"That about does it for today." Daniel propped his feet on an empty chair across from him. "Any questions?"

"Yes," said Cork, "but not about the Red Sea."

"What, then?"

"What's that?" Cork pointed to something that looked like a red plastic dish tucked away behind a cupboard.

"This?" Daniel walked over, took the disc, and held it up to them. Jude looked at Cork. Cork nodded. "Well...God forbid I let you go today without playing your first game of Frisbee."

Frisbee actually turned out to be fun. Though Jude was no better at hand-eye coordination than he'd ever been, Daniel and Cork just laughed good-naturedly at his attempts to catch, and Cork was having just as much trouble throwing it as he was. After about twenty minutes, once Jude was warm from effort even in the frosty air, Daniel went into make a phone call.

"You boys keep playing, though."

"How long can we stay?" asked Cork.

Daniel made a hand gesture as if to say, "As long as you want!" and disappeared inside.

Jude took the Frisbee and tried to make it fly in Cork's direction, but it hit the side of the house instead. Cork threw it back to him, and Jude grabbed at the air, just missing it.

"I'll get it!" said Jude. "Try again!"

Cork did try again. Jude missed again.

"Is it harder?" Cork asked. "With one hand?"

Jude paused. "I don't think so. I didn't play like this before, back home, so I don't know what it's like with two."

Cork tilted his head to the side. "Hey, are you ever going to tell me—"

"What happened?" Jude tossed the Frisbee again. This time it gently glided into Cork's hand. "I didn't know you wanted to know."

"You're my only amputee friend. Why wouldn't I want to know?"

There was that word again. *Friend.* It didn't seem as scary as it used to, but still he proceeded with caution. "I...cut it off."

Cork's eyes bulged. "*You* cut it off?"

"It was a choice—my hand or my life. I was in prison, but I hadn't done anything. I thought I was getting out. But I overheard them talking...they were going to kill me instead. Miss Shepherd heard it too, and she helped me out. But they caught us, and my chip was still implanted deep in my hand."

"So you cut it off? With what?"

"A kitchen knife."

"Holy moly."

"What?"

"You're just..." Cork's voice trailed off. Jude cringed. So much for friendship. Jude knew what he was, once again, in Cork's eyes. A weirdo. Someone to be avoided, mocked, and bullied. He wasn't prepared for the next phrase.

"You're just amazing!"

Jude swelled and caught the Frisbee as it came cutting through the yard.

They went on like that for a little while, not talking, just volleying back and forth, slowing getting better at their new game. Jude wondered what he'd be if he'd grown up in another country, or another time. Playing a game with a friend. Would it be normal, or would it still be special? He'd probably have a lot more experience at it, and at this feeling in general. Lightness. Happiness. Metrics sure did mess up a lot of things for people.

Jude had forgotten his notebook back at Daniel's, so he went back before dinner. This time, Daniel noticed his shoes.

"Nice trainers. Are they new?"

"To me, yes. They gave them to me this morning. They say next they're going to try to find a new pair of glasses for me."

"Yeah," said Daniel, lifting his eyebrows. "I can see a little crack."

"That was from where I fell looking for Samara and Denver before the airship left. I didn't even notice it for a few days after that. It would have been nice if I'd gotten them today, but these shoes are..." He paused, knowing he should appear grateful. "Nice."

"Why d'ya need glasses today if you didn't even notice the crack?"

"Well, I used to get presents every year on my birthday. From my parents."

Daniel's jaw softened and his eyes narrowed in on Jude. "It's your birthday?"

"I'm twelve today."

"I'm sorry you can't be with your parents."

"It's okay. Actually, it wasn't so great living with them. They just always got me presents every year and left them in my room. They didn't even want to be there to open them with me. And it's kind of fitting that I get these shoes today, because well...they're nice but they're not my style. And that's how it goes on this day—I get things that look like they were meant for someone else."

"Let me see those glasses." Daniel reached across the table.

Jude handed them over. Daniel turned them over in his hand. "Can you see without them?" he asked.

"Yes. Just not optimally."

Daniel smiled. Jude cringed and knew he had done that thing again; before prison, he'd never interacted with any lower tiers and found out quickly that they didn't speak quite like he did. He imagined it might be the same here, but without the official labels of the tier system.

"Let's go," said Daniel. "I'm off today. We'll drop those off with the rest of the gang up there at Olympic Village, then we'll go to the eye doctor. I'll treat you to a new pair myself."

His smile felt a little more vulnerable somehow without his glasses on his face to provide some sort of barrier between him and the world, but he smiled anyway. "Okay."

Shortly before they arrived at the optometrists' office, Jude remembered something. "I don't have health insurance here."

"Have what?"

"Health insurance. I don't have any way to pay for the exam. And the lenses will probably be really expensive." Jude shrunk, wishing he'd thought of this before now.

"I don't think you're completely covered under the National Health Service, but it shouldn't be too expensive. Once you grow up and become a permanent resident, you'll just pay your taxes and get your healthcare free when you need it."

For all the back-patting they did at Metrics for being the greatest society the world had ever seen, there were sure lots of things they hadn't thought about. Since he'd learned about it last year, Jude had wondered how lower tiers paid for health insurance for their parents between the ages of 65-75, when the rate was ten times higher than it was at any other age.

Scotland seemed, at times, to be completely different from the United States, yet when they stepped into the shop, familiarity washed over Jude. He was surrounded, as he was every year, by walls filled with frames and pictures of models in glasses—though these people had multi-colored faces, not just the new-race skin tone—looking happy and trendy in their new glasses. Even the smell was the same as it was in optometry clinics in America. The scent of carpet cleaner and glass spray made the room seem assuredly clean. Daniel cleared his throat and headed for the front desk. "Right," he said. "Is anyone available for an eye exam today? My little friend needs a new pair of glasses. Today's his birthday." Daniel said the last part just above a whisper, as if not quite sure it was the truth.

"Are you the father?" the woman asked.

"I'm from America," said Jude, and several heads turned his direction. Now he knew why Daniel had lowered his voice.

The woman's face was kind. "We'll see what we can do. We normally don't take walk-ins, but since it's your birthday..."

Jude had a feeling that wasn't the reason why she was making an exception, but he went along with it. Soon, he was sitting in a chair looking at letters of various sizes through different lenses.

"Read the bottom line, please," said the doctor when he'd gone through all the others.

"D, E, F, P, O, T, E, C."

The doctor took away the frames and slid back. "How long have you been wearing glasses, young man?"

"Since I can remember. I think I got my first pair when I was three."

"And you've had an eye exam every year?"

"Yes."

"Very strange," the doctor muttered, and turned to Daniel. "There's nothing wrong with his eyes. He has perfect vision. I'm not even sure these are prescription lenses." He took Jude's old blue frames and held them up to the light. "They may just be glass."

"I don't need to wear glasses?"

"You don't."

Jude felt oddly embarrassed, as if he should have somehow known this before now. "I'm sorry I wasted your time," he told Daniel as soon as they had left. He carried his old blue glasses in his hand, resisting the urge to put them on anyway to just feel the comfort of the weight on his face.

"It's not your fault."

"I don't know why they would have done that."

"I do," said Daniel. "Your parents probably thought they were doing what was best for you, giving you a leg up at school or whatever. But don't forget, the Ones own all the private business, and they're out to make as much money as possible. If health insurance, exams, and glasses are all expensive enough, why would they tell you there's no need to buy them?"

"But the optometrists aren't Ones. They're Threes."

"Wouldn't matter. I'll bet my front teeth they've been told to prescribe glasses to anyone who walks through the doors."

Jude gritted his teeth. "Bullshit!"

Daniel looked at him quizzically. "You don't think so?"

"No. I'm mad because I think you're right." He looked at the sidewalk, which became a blur of gray and brown as they walked. "I had a friend who used to say that when he was mad."

"You're looking for a stronger one. I think the word you're looking for," said Daniel, "is *fuck*."

"Fuck?"

"Yep. Say it loud now. *Fuck!*"

"Fuck!" That did feel good.

"Fuck!"

"Fuck!"

CHAPTER TWENTY-FOUR

SAMARA FOLLOWED THE CROWD INTO THE SQUARE, FOLLOWING behind a group of journalists. In another twenty minutes, a conservative member of Parliament would give a speech here in this suburb outside the city. It had taken Samara all morning to get here. She'd borrowed bus fare from an aid worker, who insisted it was a gift, but Samara took debts seriously. She'd pay it back when all this was over and she was a permanent resident of Scotland, or any country who'd have her free from threat of expulsion. Taye had offered to come with her, but she didn't want to ask for twice the amount she already owed for his bus ride. No, she'd manage just fine by herself.

She did her best to fit in, though the truth was that she stood out from the people here in every way possible. Luckily, the main superficial difference—the fact that all these people were quite pale—wasn't totally noticeable, as the day was cold and every body was bundled. Though the calendar said it was spring and emphasized it with a picture of blooming flowers, outside it was still necessary to cover everything except faces. Every year except this year, she looked forward to the warmer weather and how it seemed to affect everyone's outlooks, but this year was different.

She could no longer assume she'd survive long enough to enjoy another sunny picnic or afternoon by the pool, and she had to be content with living day by day. And besides, maybe it just never got warm here anyway. None of the people in the square seemed particularly annoyed by the chilly wind. Maybe they'd gotten used to it. Maybe she'd have to get used to it, too.

A man bumped her, and though she was standing still, she muttered an apology.

"Yikes, Shepherd," said a familiar voice. "You don't have to be sorry for living."

Taye stood behind Samara. If her shoulders hadn't been aching from carrying her backpack around all morning, she might have hugged him. The people around her didn't seem exactly agitated right now, but their rabble-rouser would soon be here, and she was glad to see someone she knew.

"What are you doing here?" she asked.

"I followed you."

She narrowed her eyes. "I took three buses to get here. Why didn't I see you?"

"Oh," he said, "I came on that." He pointed to a small motorbike parked on the far side of the square.

"You drove that thing here? Where'd you get it?"

"A friend loaned it to me."

"There's that knack for making friends again. What does this one want? What's the price of driving this friend's motorbike twenty miles outside the city in the freezing cold?"

Taye clicked his tongue. "You can act like you're still mad at me for not knowing that the Scots actually read books, but it turned out to be a help to our cause. So why not trust me?"

"That was lucky for you," said Samara, but she was smiling.

"Nah, I have good instincts. My mom always said so. And let me take that." He slid her backpack down her arms and onto his own back. "Oh my God, what do you have in here?"

"Raw materials. I'm going to build myself a castle."

Taye unzipped the bag and took out a book. His fingers barely fit around it. "*A Brief History of Scotland.*" He dropped it back inside. "I wouldn't want to see the unabridged version."

"It's important to know your history."

"Those who don't know their history are doomed to repeat it."

"Yes, that's what they say."

"But those who *do* know their history have to sit around chewing on their nails while they watch everyone else repeat it." He swung his arms through the straps, keeping the backpack on the front of his body. "I don't know how you wore this on your back the whole time. It hurts *my* back just to think about it."

Samara snickered and glanced back up to the empty podium. She wanted to tell Taye that the speech would be starting soon, but before she had a chance, she became aware of a group of men staring at her and Taye. Only they weren't just staring; they were seething. With their arms crossed, they shifted their weight back and forth as if they were preparing to strike. They took turns looking their way, spitting on the ground, and gritting their teeth. They were too far away to pick up any words, but whatever they were saying was tinged with a growl.

"Taye?"

"I see them. That's why I came. This is a Monroe Macintosh rally—did you really think the people here would be happy to see us?"

The crowd erupted in cheers as the man of the hour stepped out of a black transport and onto the little bandshell. He took his time, waving and smiling, before shuffling some papers on the podium. The journalists in front of Samara and Taye raised their cameras. Two raised their watches to record his speech. Seeing people with watches in Scotland was rare enough that Samara never expected it. The surprise always hit her just a minute too late, as if her brain was telling her that all was normal, all was well, just before jolting her back into reality.

"My friends!" said Macintosh, and the crowd stopped their yelling and leaned in to listen. "I can't tell you how pleased I am to see such a gratifying turnout. Together, I know you and I can reclaim Scotland for *our* people!"

Taye stepped half an inch closer to her, and Samara stepped a full inch away. She was a grownup, and this is what she expected. And if Daniel and the rest of the Red Sea trusted her enough to go to this rally alone, then she could handle it alone.

Macintosh continued, "You see all these terrible things happening in the news: the unstable United States sending its people here without any thought to how this might affect our resources and revenues. And these people are quite unlike the hard-working, brave, proud people of Scotland."

Taye groaned. "We escaped an oppressive system and somehow survived a mass murder by the government, but we're not hard-working or brave or proud or anything. Nope."

One of the journalists turned her head slightly to bring her ear closer to their conversation.

"Not so loud," Samara whispered.

"And now," said Macintosh, his voice gathering nourishment from the sounds of approval in the crowd, "We have one of them who is painting his ugly symbols of his own political thoughts on the walls of Edinburgh. Just walk around the city! You can't walk two blocks without seeing this graffiti, put up by a foreigner who wishes to brainwash our people with American propaganda!"

"Throw them out!" the men beside Samara started chanting. "Throw them out! Throw them out!"

One of the men lunged at Samara. "Throw them out on their brown asses!"

Taye threw his arm in front of Samara, and the man, who might have mistaken it for an aggressive gesture, punched Taye in the stomach. Taye stumbled backward, but the man who hit him howled in pain—instead of Taye's stomach, his fist had hit *A Brief History of Scotland*. The media was suddenly upon them, many of them pointing their cameras and watches on Taye.

Samara heard the words *did you see what he did to him* somewhere in the crowd, but she didn't know which *him* was which, and had a nasty feeling they weren't talking about the man who'd thrown the first punch. Another man from behind him took Taye's jaw in his hand and hit him, close-fisted, across his face. A flash of an old camera coincided with the sound of the strike. Samara threw her arms around Taye and dragged him away as the others leered for them both. She went through the journalists, who gave them a wide berth as they limped away as quick as they could. Taye found his feet, and the crowd cheered as they broke into a run, away from the square and down the nearest street.

Taye coughed. "The motorbike—"

"We'll get it later. Don't worry about it now."

"I have to make sure it's okay. It's not mine."

"I know. Now, shut up and let me look at you." Samara stepped in front of him and lifted her chin to look at his face. "Not too bad. The blood makes it look worse than it is."

"Very reassuring."

"Let's walk round for a little while, then we can go back and let Nurse Sue take a look."

"Nah, I'll go straight to the aid workers. They'll have the medical stuff Nurse Sue will need anyway..."

"They'll also have questions. I think we should be more strategic about who we involve in all this and when."

Taye said nothing, which Samara took as an agreement, and they walked around the little village. Surprisingly large homes loomed; not as large as they could get in the United States— Samara had been in Two neighborhoods before. She'd originally mistaken the homes there for hotels. As they walked on, Samara was amazed that these people were so fearful; they seemed to have everything, and yet they were still afraid that even a small part of it would be taken from them. And that fear was enough to compromise the lives of human beings.

"Can I ask you something?" Taye asked suddenly.

"You just did."

"Stop. That's what I—why do you always have to be right about everything? Why is every idea I have the wrong one until you decide it's right?"

"Are you still talking about the book?"

"Not just that, but yes, the book was a bad idea until you reconsidered. So was me coming with you today. And in case you wondered, I haven't told you what I've swapped for the motorbike yet because I know you'll just shoot it down. Why can't you trust that other people have ideas of their own?"

Samara gaped at him, but only for a moment since the weather insisted on constant movement. All this moving irritated her. "I'm just...I'm tired of making things up as I go along. What I really want is for someone to tell me what to do! I just want to feel safe again."

"Like you felt safe under Metrics?" Taye asked, his voice quiet and his words slurred by his swollen jaw.

"Yes! When I thought they were just out to protect me and give me a suitable life for my tier, it was actually pretty nice! Now I have to question everything before I act. Do you think I like being this way? It's exhausting."

They both turned their faces toward the pavement again, walking quickly but aimlessly down the row of beautiful homes. Samara sighed.

"What was it?"

"What?"

"What did you swap for the motorbike?"

He touched his lips before he spoke. "I promised I'd get your boyfriend to paint a canvas for this guy down at the Plum Tree. He thinks Bristol's about to become the next big thing in the art world."

CHAPTER TWENTY-FIVE

DENVER HAD BEEN HERE BEFORE. EVERY MORNING THIS WEEK, she'd awoken the same way she'd gone to sleep: in an empty bed. She could tell that Stephen had been there because of the ruffled bedclothes and the scent of him still on them, but as she doubled her time spent asleep, he halved his own.

She knew he was working on a plan with the Red Sea, but she didn't know what it was. The last time she'd witnessed him overworking, he'd been disguising his work as games on his watch to make her believe that he wasted his days playing video games when actually he was working to gather information about the relocation and lead Unregistered citizens, including her brother, to freedom. At that time, he'd been hiding his work from her to protect her—she was working for Metrics while she was finishing her studies—but there was no reason to hide his activities now. So what was going on?

She'd hardly seen him all week, and the time never seemed quite right to ask. He'd eat dinner with all of them in the dining hall and give her a peck on the cheek before inhaling his meal and taking off again in the direction of the library, Daniel's house, or Parliament. Samara insisted she didn't know what he was doing, but that the Red Sea was trusting him with something important.

Important was one thing, but dangerous was another. Denver needed to keep Stephen around, not only for sentimental reasons, but for practical ones as well; he was about to become to father of her child. He couldn't go on risking his life as usual.

After dinner that evening, she rose from the table with him when he'd finished his meal.

"I don't want to rush you," he said.

"You're not. I want to come with you tonight."

"I'll be pretty late."

"I'll come back if I get tired. I don't mind."

Stephen looked uncomfortable, but he couldn't force her to stay and he knew it. She'd already brought her coat down from their room and pulled it on. She was already getting thick around the middle. She didn't yet look like an expectant mother, but she didn't look or feel like her normal self, either. She zipped her coat with some difficulty and followed him out the door. Either she was also getting slower, or he was walking abnormally fast. She struggled to keep up as he weaved through streets and alleyways.

"Just in case we're being followed," he said over his shoulder.

They eventually came to a university. The brick building's facade was imposing, especially in the half-light of dusk, and the steps leading up the door were steep. Denver was winded by the third one, but continued to the top. Stephen stopped at the door and waited for her.

"Stephen," she said, winded, "what is this?"

"Training." He barely moved his mouth when he said it, yet his eyes were actively searching her.

"Oh. What are we being trained on?"

"We're not being trained on anything. We're the ones doing the training."

She waited for him to explain, but he just walked through the door and down the hall. She made an involuntary growling nose in her throat and followed.

Eventually, he stopped and held a classroom door open for her. About twenty people held their own conversations among each other in desks facing the front of the room. Daniel was there, too, along with a woman Denver recognized from TV—someone from Parliament. She and Daniel were chatting and greeted Stephen warmly when they saw him. When Denver walked in, neither of them bothered to hide their surprise.

"Mrs. Steiner?" asked Daniel. "Nice to see you again!" His eyes traveled conspicuously from her face to her belly and back again.

"It's Denver," she said. "Nice to see you, too. And I don't believe we've met." She reached a hand out to the woman whom she knew by sight but not by name.

The woman shook it. "Melinda Terry. I am so glad you decided to join us tonight. Your insight will be very valuable."

"I'm sorry, but I don't know exactly—"

"Let's get started," Stephen said and cleared his throat loudly enough to stop the ambient voices. The people in the seats, Denver noticed for the first time, were not the usual white Scots that she was now used to seeing, but mixed-race, like herself.

"As usual, we'll do the culture part of training first, then Daniel and Melinda will take over for strategy discussions. Tonight, we'll start with practicing our American accents. We'll practice having a conversation with our partners about popular TV shows. We'll do these first as Twos, and then as Threes, and then as Fours. Did everyone bring the slang cheat sheets from last week?" Several held up copied paper sheets. Denver felt her heart rate quicken in her veins as Stephen's plan dawned on her. "That's great. Let's get started."

———

After Stephen's portion, the class took a bathroom break. She leaned in to Daniel and Melinda. "I'm getting tired, but I don't want to walk home alone. Would you mind if I stole Stephen back to walk me home?"

"Of course not!" said Daniel. "We'll muddle through without him tonight."

"See you tomorrow night, Mr. Steiner," said Melinda.

Denver thanked them and gave Stephen a sharp look. They walked away together in silence until they were out of earshot. Instead of following the hallway back outside, Denver led him into an empty classroom and shut the door.

"What the hell is going on, Stephen?"

He sighed and sunk into a chair, deflated. "The justice department here has a plan to liberate the United States. They obviously won't tell me all of it, but they asked me to help."

"They asked? Or you volunteered?"

"They asked."

"Why you?"

"Maybe because I've been working for the Red Sea since I was a teenager!"

Denver hadn't heard him snap like that before. She wanted to snap back, but she needed him to open up, so she softened her face. "Just tell me what's going on. I'm entitled to that much."

He rubbed his shoulder with his opposite hand. "Those people in there are the UK's spies. They're going to the US in a few months to infiltrate Metrics. Like I said, I don't know the whole plan, but I hope they can overthrow Metrics and give the US its democracy back. It's been a long time coming, and we can be a part of it." His eyes were wide and pleading. "I know the timing's not right, but I didn't choose it."

"Why now?"

"It's the Bird. He knows we're here, and he's working with the UK to provide an insider connection to Metrics. He usually addresses the group by hologram at the end of these meetings. Us coming here might be the key to liberating the US."

Denver pursed her lips and looked down at the floor. Little specks of purple and yellow were randomly splattered on each tile; an homage to fashionable interior decorating of the previous decade. "You're planning on going with them."

"I haven't decided yet." His voice was hoarse. "I do have to go to London next week to start training the rest."

"Were you going to tell me?"

"Of course." He stood, took her hands, and pressed them against his forehead. "I just hadn't found the right time."

"Tell them I'm coming with you."

He nodded his head slowly at first, then with more conviction. "I think we can do that. I'll tell them that you can help. You know the Threes much better than me, and most of these people are going into Three positions—"

"I'm going to London with you, yes. But I'm also going back with you, if that's your choice."

Blood drained from Stephen's face. Denver planted herself firmly and watched him, almost enjoying his trepidation. *Serves him right.*

"You can't."

"I can."

"You would put our child in danger?"

"Our child has always been in danger. It's the air he breathes now. I won't let you go alone."

Stephen stared at the ground for a long time, not moving except to blink. Samara continued to watch him, enjoying it less with every passing moment. Finally, he said, "We'll go to London together. I do think you can help if you want. And I'll talk to some of the others about finding a replacement to go back with the recruits. I can gamble with life; I can even afford to lose someone else's, if it came to that. But yours, and our baby's..."

Denver closed her eyes and pressed her fingertips on them. It did feel different now. Bristol had always depended on her somewhat, but it was nothing like this new life. Still, was it fair to tell someone else they had to go instead?

"When do we leave?"

"Monday morning."

It would be their first train ride together since the trip they took on the hospital express when they escaped Metrics. This time, though, it would probably be her, not Stephen, who would be sick to her stomach.

CHAPTER TWENTY-SIX

BRISTOL LOOKED OVER HIS ITINERARY FOR THE DAY. HE HAD AN interview with an art magazine at ten, and then a lunch meeting with a gallery owner. After that, it was back to Olympic Village to work a bit, and finally a cocktail reception in the evening. Though the agent who'd met him and Samara at the Scottish Museum of Contemporary art had been kind and asked him to think over her offer for a few weeks, she'd called every day afterward to push him into signing a contract with her. Samara seemed happy with her persistence and told him it would be good for the cause, so Bristol had accepted on the third day. Now, only a few days later, she was concerned less with his art and their cause and her eyes sparkled when she talked, and she talked of nothing but his *career*.

Career. Bristol never thought to have one of those. Even back home, when he thought about what it might be like to be assigned as an artist, he'd guffaw at the absurdity. Back home, though, artists didn't paint what they liked; they made things for city parks or the homes of rich citizens. The really famous ones painted portraits of the Ones, which he'd seen only once at the library. His new agent, Cindy, insisted it was different here. He could make anything he wanted. In fact, the raunchier, the better. He didn't think he'd ever had the urge to paint anything raunchy, but it felt good to know he could if he wanted. And he wouldn't even have to tie a pack of ice around his wrist to do it.

Samara stepped into the common room with two mugs of black coffee. The mere scent of it gave him a feeling of grounding and warmth.

"They don't serve breakfast this early."

"You're right; they don't," said Samara, setting one cup down. "It's instant. I snuck into the kitchen."

Bristol smiled and wrapped his hands around one of the white ceramic mugs. "What are you doing up?"

"Hoping to catch you. Jude said you'd been waking up before the sun."

"I just need some time alone to work."

"Oh," said Samara, and rummaged through her bag. "I can...I brought a book in case you didn't want to talk."

"No, that's not what I meant. I can talk."

She smiled and curled her legs underneath her on the vinyl sofa. "Okay," she said. "How does it feel to have a *career?*" She imitated Cindy's pronunciation of the word *career,* and even pulsed her eyes a little wider at the beginning of it, as his new agent always did.

Bristol chuckled into his coffee. "It's not real yet. And it feels a little bit like I'm selling something that's not meant to be sold. It's not a big deal, what I do. Anyone could do it. You could do it."

"Maybe. But I don't. That's probably the difference. You actually took the steps to do it, to teach yourself. And you're not selling your pieces for yourself."

"They're paying me."

"I mean the real reason you're doing it is to get the public on our side. To get us to stay in Scotland." She raised her eyebrows. "Aren't you?"

"Yes, of course."

"And I know not all of them are paying you." She looked down, and Bristol's shoulder's rose.

"You mean that thing I had to do for Taye?" He sighed. "No, that was worth it."

"He traded one of your paintings for a motorbike ride."

The contempt in her voice sent a thrill through Bristol, though he tried not to let it show. "He told me what he did for you at the rally. I wish I'd thought to be there with you, but I'm glad someone was. It's definitely worth a stupid canvas to know that you could have been hurt but weren't."

Samara fidgeted. "I would have been fine. Men bring out the worst in other men."

"Still," said Bristol, "you aren't planning to go to any more of those, are you?"

"Bristol, I have to gather information."

"The news already does that."

She snorted. "Sure, trust the media. They told us they were sending you to Arizona!"

"The *Metrics* media lies, yes."

"What if it's the same here? What would you rather do—put all of our trust in them or actually go and double-check that the information they're giving us is correct?" She didn't wait for him to answer. "I know what I would rather do."

Bristol took a long sip. Taye was right—in their one and only conversation yesterday, he'd asked if Samara had always been this way, and Bristol knew what he meant without having to ask. She had become obsessed with finding truth and delivering justice. She only trusted others to do small things for her, and she insisted on doing the rest. All this mistrust was beginning to take a toll physically. Her cinnamon curls had become dry and frayed. Her cheeks were red and chapped, and her lips, though still pink, were cracked. Dark circles hovered under her once-bright eyes.

"What time did you go to bed last night, Samara?"

"What does that have to do with anything?"

"We're not living under Metrics anymore. You don't get rewarded for working your life away and not taking care of yourself. You look like you got about four hours." Truthfully it looked more like two, but Bristol hoped otherwise. "I'm not saying you can't do your best to help, but you need to take it down a notch. Let other people share the work. If you don't trust the journalists, spend time getting to know them. Find out their motivation and who pays them. Then, maybe you can let them do some of this for you so you can focus on more important things."

"Like what?"

"Like finding out what Jude's up to." He took a longer drink of his coffee, grateful that it was cooling off. "Or Stephen. Or Denver, for that matter."

"Jude's fine."

"Jude's *not* fine. He's getting angry again, like he was at Nan's. He's becoming fanatical about Daniel, and he's not sleeping much either."

"Is *anyone* sleeping enough for you? Denver seems to get enough. Can't you be happy with that?"

He bristled. "Denver is packing right now, did you know that?"

He could see she didn't. She looked at him and spoke softly. "Where is she going?"

"She and Stephen are going to London today to train some spies that are going to pose as Americans. And I suspect they're thinking of doing something crazy like joining them. This is what I'm talking about; the Red Sea is using us—"

"To liberate our home!"

"Yes, but they're not concerned with us as a unit. They're just picking us off to do their bidding, and no one's keeping us all informed of the bigger picture." He leaned in and put his elbows on his knees. "That's what we really need. Someone with sound mental abilities to draw us together."

Samara squeezed her eyes shut. "I don't know if I meet those qualifications. Sound mental abilities."

"No, right now, you don't. But if you can let the media do its job, and focus on leading us, then we might have a shot." He leaned back into the green vinyl. "And I think it's time that everybody knew what we were doing, not just those of us who were at Daniel's house that first night."

"But all of us won't fit in Daniel's living room."

"Then we'll have meetings here."

"Here? The aid workers might hear us."

"Let them."

Samara thought, and Bristol saw that it wasn't easy for her. He knew what it was like, having one's brain functions impaired by lack of rest. He could see the cogs struggling to turn in her mind, rusty and sluggish. "Samara," he said, putting his coffee cup down. "Go back to bed for a few hours. When you wake up, you'll be ready to think about this some more."

"I wanted to go with you to do the interview. In case you need help with your talking points."

"I'll wake you before I go."

Samara reluctantly agreed and shuffled upstairs. He was glad she no longer had her watch to distract her. Here, if she wanted to catch up on the news she didn't trust, she had to be in the common room.

He missed her as soon as she left. He looked at a fresh page, waiting for his drawing. He took another drag of coffee, but it had turned cold.

CHAPTER TWENTY-SEVEN

DENVER SAT IN A GRAY SEAT WITH A TALL BACK. SCOTLAND often seemed like a crummier version of home, with its outdated technology and its starchy food, but today she was impressed; its trains were demonstrably better. There was more than enough room for her to stretch out her legs, which surprised her because everything else here—the refrigerators, the closets, even the money—had seemed so tiny compared to what she was used to. There was a little tray where she set her book. One of the aid workers had let her borrow a book about pregnancy, and everything she'd read so far had been fascinating. But she didn't particularly want to read today; she'd much rather just look out the window.

Stephen seemed to want the same thing because he placed his own book beside hers, took her hand, and leaned over her lap to get a better view. The only thing they could see right now was the inside of the train station, with people busily walking to their trains, or waiting, or eating, or, in one case, busking. Denver squeezed her husband's hand and focused her eyes on the man with the instrument, one they didn't have in America. The only kind of musicians there were the ones assigned to the role. They'd never play in a train station.

"That's called a guitar. Daniel told me," said Stephen.

"It doesn't look familiar, but it seems like I've heard it before."

"I think we have. When the pop songs come out in the spring, there's usually a guitar somewhere in the mix."

Denver smiled slightly as she recalled. Of course, now that he'd said that, she could place it—in one of her favorite songs, "Silence Makes my Life Sing," there was a long guitar interlude in the middle. Most songs had the same structure: verse, pre-chorus, chorus, verse, pre-chorus, chorus, bridge, chorus. This one surprised her by extending the bridge. She didn't know much at all about music, so she didn't know how long they'd extended it, but she recognized the difference and respected the unnamed musicians. They must have fought for that.

She and Stephen held hands and watched the guitarist play until the train moved, not with a jerk and a tug like trains did back home, but with a smooth glide away from the station. They stayed with their eyes glued out the window as they watched the city whiz past the glass. Finally, only when they had left the city and sheep had begun to dot the grassy hills outside, Stephen broke away and reached for his book.

Denver stopped him with small talk. "Did they tell you anything about London?"

He snapped his book shut again and turned to her with bright eyes. "They gave me instructions on how to get to our hotel. There'll be someone there to help us check in."

In spite of the looming cloud of possibility in the air, she was excited to stay somewhere different. She'd never been to a hotel before. Back home, only Twos were allowed to travel overnight, so she'd never even thought it would be a possibility. They talked about how quickly their lives had changed, how surreal it seemed even now, weeks after they'd arrived in this new country. Denver laughed and savored the feeling of her lips stretching over her teeth, the pull at her abdomen. She wasn't in the habit of laughing.

If Stephen stayed here and they found new volunteers to go back, maybe she could get used to it.

When the train pulled into the station again, they marveled at the size of it all—everything seemed larger than life, and, in scale, they were so small. There were more people who looked like them, too, which made Denver feel slightly more comfortable despite her new surroundings. They took another, smaller train that ran underground to their hotel, and when they got there, a giddy young man with skin like early morning met them to show them to their room.

"They didn't tell you *anything?*" he asked them again in the elevator. He'd insisted on carrying both of their bags, but they didn't seem to be weighing him down. On the contrary, he looked ready to fly away. Any second now, he'd hover over the floor like a hologram. "You really thought that the whole world was under your government's control?"

"You know, there may be things you don't know that seem obvious to other people," Denver said, knowing she sounded sassy and the man was just excited. Still, she wished people would stop acting like they should have known they'd been lied to their entire lives. "They tell all citizens there that Metrics is a worldwide government. From birth, that's what we're told. There wasn't a reason to think otherwise."

The man carried their bags to a door marked 517. "Your prints will open it," he said.

Denver looked at Stephen, hoping he knew what that meant. But Stephen just looked back at her.

"Fingerprints," the man clarified, wise enough now to not show amusement at their ignorance.

Denver pressed the pads of her fingers into a little screen. A green light flashed, and there was a clicking sound.

Stephen shook the man's hand. "Will we be seeing you again?"

"Yes, I expect we'll see much more of each other. Tomorrow morning, for one. I'm part of the team going back with you two."

Denver pressed her teeth together, but Stephen seemed unfazed. "Ah. See you tomorrow morning, then."

Despite the darker jewel tones of the walls and bedspread, the open windows brightened up the room. Denver felt the urge to draw the curtains, drown out the light, and lock the door from the inside. She wanted to hole herself up and tell anyone who came to get them that they were never coming out again, to just leave them in peace. Was that too much to ask for? Just a little *peace*?

Stephen bounced playfully on the bed, totally oblivious. "Nice and springy. Want to try?"

"Not now."

"What's wrong?"

"My stomach hurts. Must have been those crisps on the train."

He got up and wrapped an arm around her. "Lie down. I'll lie with you."

"No thanks. It's a restless sick." She walked to the window and scanned the city skyline. "What's that?"

"I don't know. It looks like a giant wheel."

"Are they building something?"

"Let's go check it out. We can walk all the way there and get dinner in a restaurant."

They'd both been excited about this. They still didn't have watches, but the government here had given them a card with money on it for meals to eat while they were away from Olympic Village. Denver's excitement had waned, the sudden gloominess of reality clouding it out. Still, she didn't want to steal Stephen's.

"Okay. Give me five minutes."

She walked into the bathroom, noting her reflection in the mirror looked a little more ashen than usual. When she wiped, there was a streak of blood on the toilet paper.

CHAPTER TWENTY-EIGHT

JUDE QUICKLY LEARNED THAT THE WORD "FUCK" WAS OKAY when one was alone, but not when one was in a crowded street, elevator, or shop. Back home, only the lower tiers used curse words. Jude was among mostly lower-tier boys at the prison, but since they weren't allowed to talk most of the time, Jude didn't get much experience with the nuances of cursing. He decided he'd only use his new word around Daniel until he figured out how to do it properly.

"Or," Daniel said, "you could try to calm down, not get so angry over things you can't control."

"You sound like my teachers," said Jude. "They were always telling us to be resilient, but what they meant was never complain, just take whatever they throw at you."

"What'd your parents say?"

"My parents didn't talk to me."

Daniel exhaled so completely that the papers on the table in front of him fluttered. "I'm not telling you to just lie down and take it. Surrender isn't always weakness. You have to learn to recognize things you can control and things you can't. Work like hell to change the things you can, curse sometimes when it helps.

Swears can be useful for releasing some of that rage, but if you use them when the rage isn't really there, or there's not enough of it to warrant the use of one, those words can just create this low-range anger that stays with you, slowing brewing. That's no way to live."

"I'm not angry *all* the time."

"Not for lack of tryin'."

"I'm getting real sick of your shit, Daniel."

"Look who learned a new one! I think in America, though, they pronounce it sh-i-t. 'I' like in 'igloo.' We're the ones who say it like sh-ai-t. Wouldn't want people to find out you were a Two back home, eh?"

Jude looked at the floor, feeling, for the first time, that slow brew stewing inside. But he wanted to get it right, just in case he needed it again. "Sh-i-t."

"That's right. At least, I think. The last time I saw a movie made in America, that's how they were saying it."

"You've seen American movies?"

"Oh, yeah. Old ones. America used to be famous for its movies." Daniel ran a hand over the back of his head. "We'll watch one sometime."

Jude recognized that he made this invitation without quite meaning to, and he was reminded of JoJo. Jude didn't particularly love spending time around his little friend, but he just somehow found himself in situations where hanging out had been his own idea. He felt sorry for him, in a way—he was just a little kid, and after all he'd been through, he needed a friend. This must have been exactly what Daniel thought of him.

Jude told Daniel that he'd love to watch an American movie sometime, but never asked for a specific time and noted that Daniel didn't either.

He walked home the long way, through the park. Being around the trees and the pond always restored him, no matter how angry he got with the way people had wrecked the world. They sure made a mess of things, but it was comforting to know that the trees and the pond were always there, and surely there would be more trees and more ponds, even if the so-called adults in charge decided to destroy these.

Across the pond, a figure caught Jude's eye. What struck him was not the way this person was dressed or what she was doing; he recognized the gait of her walk: Samara. It wasn't unusual at all; lots of the refugees spent hours here in this park—with little to do at Olympic Village, most of them braved the cold for an afternoon stroll. Jude just tugged at the corners of his jacket, content to let her pass. He didn't want to be an annoyance to *two* adults today. He was just beginning to feel sorry for himself, seeing his pitiful self through their eyes, a little kid, woefully misinformed and dragging down their grownup conversations, when he noticed Samara wasn't just walking, she was pacing.

It was like the pacing he sometimes saw in the Fox County Detention Center, where he'd been kept for months before Samara helped him escape. Some inmates lost control of their minds temporarily, or at least that's what Kopecky told him. In the prison yard, they'd make little paths in the dirt, walking back and forth to calm themselves until a guard came with their injection. The injection was scarier than the pacing. Their eyes would go glassy, their mouths would hang open, and their feet would be so still that they'd need help moving to another room. Jude knew Samara had transformed in the short time they'd been in Scotland, and not for the better, but had she changed that much? Was she losing control?

He wanted to believe that she hadn't, so he hung back. He was tired of talking to people anyway. It was true that he sought out Daniel every day, but all this talk was draining his energy. He'd come to the park for a little peace and quiet, after all.

After several minutes, it became clear that Samara hadn't lost her marbles after all. She was waiting for someone. That someone showed up in a long, black transport. Without seeing the front of it, he could tell it had a human driver—it was too shiny to be a driverless car. The driver was hidden, though, behind the black-mirror windows. Samara looked over both shoulders before she slipped inside. He was too far away to see who was inside, but his imagination ran wild with speculation. Jude suddenly feared for Samara's safety and ran across the pedestrian bridge to get closer, not knowing what he might do if he were to catch the car. Though the car moved slowly through the park, he was too far away, and painfully out of shape. He squeezed his side to relieve a jab that appeared after seconds of running and slowed down slightly. By that time, the transport was at the park's entrance with its right turn signal blinking. "Hey!" said Jude aloud in the car's direction. "Hey!" People were staring. Jude started to run again, but by the time he'd broken into a real sprint again, the car had turned and was gliding down the street, quick as a bird in flight.

Jude stopped, panting on the sidewalk. He wanted to tell these people looking at him to fuck off, but he didn't have enough breath for that. Instead, he tried assuring himself that Samara was a grown woman who could take care of herself and surely knew what she was doing. He told himself that Daniel would know what she was up to, and that he'd probably arranged this meeting himself. But the more he tried arguing with himself, the stronger the opposite voice became; there was something funny about this. He didn't like it and he wouldn't, no matter how long he stood here trying to convince himself otherwise. He thought for a moment about going back to Daniel's, but instead, he went back to Olympic Village. He'd have to ask Daniel what he knew about this, but first he wanted to connect with someone he was sure would be more worried than he was, just to know he wasn't crazy.

CHAPTER TWENTY-NINE

THE JACKET HAD BARELY MADE IT OVER BRISTOL'S SHOULDERS before he stepped in front of the bathroom mirror. The clothes that Cindy had dropped off for tonight were easily the nicest he'd ever worn. Gone were the days of wearing an orange vest over his kitchen blacks, signaling to the world he was allowed to be out past curfew because he cooked for his betters all day and stayed late to clean their messes. Standing in front of his mirror tonight, he admired his gray tweed suit. He liked the way it speckled without shimmering—it reminded him of cement, like the kind he and Denver used to draw on outside their building with sidewalk chalk in the summer. Under the jacket, he wore a plum shirt and dark navy tie. There was a little accessory Cindy called a tie bar, but he couldn't figure it out and he didn't think he needed it anyway. He'd never felt ugly the way Denver bemoaned that she did; he'd never really thought about the way he looked before. But he was thinking about it now. And he was thinking he looked undeniably good, tie bar or no tie bar.

Cindy, who'd been waiting in the hallway, gasped and clapped her hands when he walked out. "Spin 'round!"

Bristol complied, but as soon as he'd made the full rotation, he noticed Cindy staring at his shoes. "Weren't the rental shoes in the bag?"

"Yeah—about that," Bristol said, digging the heel of one of his ripped, worn kitchen shoes into the floor, "I was thinking I could wear these instead."

"What's the matter with the rentals? Too shiny? I could get suede instead."

"No," said Bristol, making a mental note to ask someone what suede was later. "It's just that I don't want people there to forget that I'm a refugee. These are the shoes I ran twenty miles in to escape Metrics. I was exiled from the monastery in these, too, for asking questions. I arrived in Scotland wearing these. If people see them and think they look out of place, I want them to consider that we're all out of place, and we need them as allies if we're ever going to fit in with them."

Cindy seemed unmoved by his speech, and waved her hand in the air. "You're the artist." That seemed to settle it. "Give me that."

She fastened his tie bar between the third and fourth buttons of his shirt, and he wondered if she needed to be quite so close to do it. It was a crazy, fleeting thought, he realized—he missed Samara. Cindy stepped back and admired him again, her eyes pulsing on words she accentuated. "Now," she said, "let's go have a *fabulous* time with some *important* people."

Bristol wanted one last look in his mirror, but he'd rather die than admit that. Instead, he and Cindy walked down the stairs to sounds of admiration, led mostly by JoJo. He glimpsed Taye, but he was sitting in the far corner of the room, pretending not to notice Bristol. Before they left, Cindy insisted they take a picture together in front of the Olympic rings still painted on the wall. She wrapped her arms around him and smiled, making it look like they were the best of friends, or maybe lovers. He was afraid he couldn't control his own facial expression, and he felt temporarily detached from his body as he looked for Samara and wondered what she would think to see Cindy hanging off of him like this. But she was nowhere. Probably out discovering information that had already been discovered by the city's hundreds of reporters. Screw it. He threw his arms around Cindy, who actually giggled as Nurse Sue snapped another picture.

They stepped outside, where a red driverless transport stood waiting for them. Inside, Cindy adjusted his tie again and whispered, "Did you ever think you'd be on your way to a reception to introduce your work to the UK?"

"I didn't know what a reception was, or that the UK existed, or that what I was doing was considered work."

"A simple no would have sufficed." She smiled at him, then out the window.

The room where the party was held was enchanting. Large glass vases held long-stemmed lilies that seemed to fawn over the beautiful people scattered throughout the room. Bristol noticed the beauty of the women first. The colors of their faces were too stunning to be real—crimson lips, rose cheeks, cerulean eyes. But the men, whose color looked much closer to reality, also had a crippling beauty about them. The lines of their faces and bodies were long and crisp and defined, and they were the ones Bristol looked forward to sketching from memory in the morning. Maybe over coffee.

"Bristol, this is Paige Dunaway," Cindy said with an airy gesture toward a woman with bright pink lips and long black hair. "She's the editor of *Modern Art Today*."

"Nice to meet you," Bristol said.

"We're *so* glad to have you here. *Thank* you for coming." Paige had the same habit of letting her eyes do the annunciating for her.

"I didn't have a choice." Bristol's comment was nothing but a true statement, but both women laughed.

"Tell her about your shoes, Bristol."

He told her about his shoes, about his journey, about how he liked Scotland so far. She and Cindy listened marvelously, reacting with theatrical expressions at just the right points. Bristol never thought to think of his life as interesting, but here, among the rich and beautiful, he was finally able to see his life as somewhat important. People kept joining their circle, nodding and leaning in to hear Bristol talk.

"My husband and I have been very impressed with your work. It's so provocative, the risk you took to make it is evident in the final product, almost visible. It must be so fulfilling to know that your art inspired so many to question their lives back where you're from," said Paige. "Especially when you had so many forces conspiring against you."

"Yes," said Bristol. He wasn't able to say any more, though, because his memory transported him without warning from this swanky room with its purple glow back to Nan's safe house in Fallwood. He hadn't known that Samara knew he'd been the one behind the graffiti, but she did know. What had she said to him? *You've shown me who you are and who I can be. I've seen the beauty inside your mind, and I fell in love with that beauty.* He wanted to kiss her, but she kissed him first. And her kiss was soft and sweet and urgent and hungry all at the same time...

Bristol snapped back when he became aware that someone in the circle had asked him a question. "Excuse me?"

"I asked, what are you working on now? If anything?"

"Oh. I'm doing some sketches of my sister."

"Your sister seems to appear in your work quite often," Paige said.

"I know her face better than anyone else's, I guess, so it's easier for me to draw. She and her husband are expecting their first child and—" there was a little gasp from the crowd around him and murmurs of congratulations. "Thank you. I'm experimenting with the ways to show how the baby inside her is free in a way we're not. The baby is without country or language or tier. Her child could belong to anyone right now. It'd be a shame to send him or her back to the USA."

"Your sister's child has a bright future in Scotland!" said someone in the back.

"And so do you!"

"And so do your people!"

"There has been much talk in Parliament about sending you all back. You must have seen the reports," said Paige. "But we won't let that happen."

Simultaneously bemused by their assumption that everything would turn out just fine—that must have been the pattern of their own lives so far—and supported by this large group of influencers, Bristol's heart beat in his ears and his palms broke into a sweat.

Cindy walked over and patted his arm. "We all have much work to do if we're going to make this world a better place for your niece or nephew. But this is a good start." Bristol looked down, wishing there was a trap door under his feet to hide him away from all this attention. "Let's get you a drink," she said.

The drink was bubbly, but bitter. Bristol poked at the ice with the little straw a few times while Cindy relayed his story of escape once again, with considerably more drama added, to another group of chiseled-looking people. Bristol took Cindy aside after she was finished and asked if they could leave now.

"Let's stay another hour," she urged. "The McColls just told me that they'd like to arrange a benefit for the American refugees."

Bristol was tired of asking her what she meant, so he just pretended to know who the McColls were and what a benefit was and agreed to stay. The drink was making him fuzzy.

A little cough caught Bristol's attention. No one else had noticed it, but it was familiar to him. He looked around, suddenly alert again. He walked out of the room and into a little corridor where Jude was standing on the other side of the door frame. Bristol smiled brightly at Jude's mangy second-hand clothes, which made him look soft and young in this light.

"What are you doing here?" he asked.

"I—it's Samara," said Jude. "She got into a black lime-o-seen at the park."

"A limousine?" Bristol asked, his brow knitted.

"Yes, a limousine. And Daniel doesn't know what she's doing. None of the Red Sea people know. And she's not back yet."

It was almost midnight. "I told her we needed to be on the same page."

"What are we going to do?"

"What she would do if it were us."

Jude nodded, his eyes much too world-weary for someone his age. Together, they stepped out into the night to find her.

CHAPTER THIRTY

ON THE PHONE, NURSE SUE TOLD DENVER TO LIE DOWN AND call her if the bleeding got worse. Stephen insisted that the nurse had meant to lie down longer than an hour and would not let her back up for the rest of the night. He brought her chicken soup and crackers for dinner.

"I'm not sick," she said. "Nurse Sue said a little bleeding can be perfectly normal."

"Just eat it so I feel better. Can I get you anything else? Chocolate? Ice cream?"

Denver smiled. Back home, as a Four, he wouldn't be allowed to buy those things for her. "Just stay here with me. We'll get some chocolate tomorrow morning before we go to the training center."

But in the morning, there was another streak of blood on her underwear, and they agreed she'd better stay in bed. Stephen looked gray when he left. He gave her the number for the training center and insisted she call immediately with any updates.

Alone, she put her hand on her stomach again.

Denver never thought to wonder what her mother had gone through the day she walked into the abortion center to end Bristol's life; she only knew that she'd discovered she was pregnant again—by a man who wasn't her husband—and walked out of the center after they told her to lie down. How far along had she been? Probably around this same time, four months of carrying her child at the same time she was caring for Denver, just barely a year old then. Denver's mother must have known what she was in for, both physically and practically; she'd been pregnant before. She'd given birth before. She knew that a second child would mean a slash to her citizenship score that she wouldn't be able to repair; that she'd be able to stay a Three, since no one ever moved tiers back then, but that life for her infant daughter would be forever changed once she was old enough to marry. Denver was ashamed of it, but she had always carried just a touch of resentment for that, that her mother would rather carry her second child to term than to sacrifice him for her future.

As she felt the familiar jab of shame for thinking, even for a moment, that her mother should have gone through with the abortion that day, she clutched her stomach. Something was coming upon her slowly, a physical sensation of twisting, grinding, inside her stomach. Cramps. She'd had some back at St. Mary's, early on. Probably nothing. She was glad when it faded away, and with it, the shame and her mother's memory.

She flipped through the newspaper that had been left by their door this morning. Her movements were restless, and her eyes firmly trudged through the headlines, forcing her mind back to the present, back to the severity of their situation here as refugees. She'd have to do a better job keeping up with the news...

It didn't take long before her gaze fuzzed over again, imagining her mother at her own age. She'd seen pictures of her from back then. She was built like Denver, long and lean. A thin waistline that would have betrayed her secret quickly. Did she have a bump under her dress the day she walked up the steps to the abortion center? Denver knew which center she'd gone to—a tall gray building downtown with steps that looked like a gauntlet. There were police on either side of those steps, supposedly to protect the women who were only allowed to go in alone. But Denver had always suspected that they were also there to keep women from running out, as her mother had done. Were they always there? The day her mother went with Bristol in her body, were they there, sneering and laughing at her?

Denver's son would someday be a full-grown person, just like Bristol was now. He no longer seemed so imaginary when she thought of it that way. Just as slowly as it had come before, a wave of stronger pain hit Denver and she could no longer pretend it was harmless. She fought against it, grasping her middle as if to protect her baby from the pain. She didn't know much about pregnancy, it was true, but it didn't seem like her baby would survive if he were to be born today. Then again, she was so ignorant of these things. Maybe he would be fine, just tiny.

Denver's mother would have gone through the doors and probably signed some papers, feeling sick, asking why the baby happened at all. Maybe feeling guilty.

Her stomach crunched in on itself again. *No.*

Did her husband know at this point? Mom was having an affair with another man, a long-term affair judging from the number of children that resulted from their relationship. Denver and Bristol's biological father—did he know?

That one was stronger.

Did she talk to Bristol as she waited in the ugly waiting room, probably dotted with vases filled with dusty silk flowers and Metrics posters assuring her that she was doing the right thing? Did she tell him she was sorry?

I'm sorry.

They'd have called her into the waiting room. They'd have told her to take off her clothes and put on a gown. It would have been cold in the room. It was always so cold wherever they made you wear a gown.

Stop. Stop, stop.

Denver clamped her teeth together to stop them from chattering and slowly lowered her legs to the floor. She waded to the bathroom and, with effort, sat on the toilet. The pain was coming fast and strong now. She fought against them as if she were standing on a beach, wrestling strong waves. Each one knocked her over, quickly weakening her. But she sensed relief was near.

She looked into the toilet. Blood-red water.

No, no. Stay with me.

They'd told her mother to lie down.

Denver got up again, trailing thick blood behind her. It was on the soles of her feet, but the pain stopped her from caring what happened to the carpet. She had to reach the phone before the next wave hit. She reached out and touched it with her fingertips. More pain. All pain. Denver pulled her hand away, leaving a red swipe across the top of it.

"She's about four months along," the doctor were saying about her mother. "Let's suck it out. Spread your legs."

Denver opened her own legs, right there on the floor beside the bed. The blood was everywhere now, the shades of red forming a spectrum between the dark, jelly-like clots on the floor and the bright watercolors on the inside of each thigh. Denver's body pushed, and she reached down and received something in her hands.

My baby.

He didn't look like a baby, but it was him. Small enough to fit in the palm of her hand, he had translucent skin and large black spots on either side of his head. He was withered, curled into a loose ball, and even through the blood, his blue veins were visible. It was him, this small manifestation of love, not done growing. Not ready to leave her.

Her mother had snapped her knees back together, grabbed her clothes, and ran back down those concrete steps, with translucent, tiny Bristol still safe in her womb.

I'm so sorry.

She held him close. The room was growing darker. Someone knocked on the door, said something, and opened it. Denver was conscious just long enough to hear a woman scream.

CHAPTER THIRTY-ONE

SAMARA TOOK TWO CUPS DOWN FROM THE CABINET, BUT ONLY shook instant coffee grounds into one of them. The sky was turning pink with the promise of a sunrise, but Bristol wasn't in the common room yet. She'd just wait for him to come down. She held her news inside her, rehearsing what she'd say when he sat down on the sofa. She'd wait for him to take a sip or two so he'd be fully awake for the best reaction. She smiled as she anticipated it; the last time she'd seen Bristol truly surprised was when she kissed him for the first time. She was sure that he'd prefer that kind of surprise again, but this one would have to do in the meantime.

She was too excited to sit down. She'd been too excited to sleep, too, though she didn't feel tired at all. It was as if an energy were animating her from the inside out, and—for now, at least—she didn't need to rely on her biochemical energy. She didn't need sleep, or food, or water, at least not right now, while the flame inside her was still burning bright.

She stood at the window, watching the birds peck the yard outside in the half-light of dawn without really seeing them. The clock on the wall revealed that it had been nearly an hour since she'd been downstairs. Where was he? With a sweep of disappointment, she remembered that he had been at the cocktail reception last night. He was probably sleeping in this morning, exhausted from rubbing shoulders with the upper crust of the art world.

Wait until he heard who she'd been talking to.

Waiting was the one thing she couldn't do. She turned to go up the steps to his room. Before she'd gotten to the first landing, however, she heard someone come in the front door.

It was Bristol and Jude. They didn't see her, and walked past the steps to the common room. She flew down the steps to follow them.

"Hey!"

They turned, and when they saw it was her, they both rushed to embrace her at the same time, resulting in a tangled jumble of arms and heads facing awkward ways. They were all three laughing, though Samara didn't know exactly what they were laughing about.

Jude pulled away and patted Samara's arms, as if to make sure she was really there. "Where were you?"

"That's a story that is much too fascinating for this hallway. Let's get some coffee and sit down." She looked at Bristol. "Nice suit, handsome."

Bristol's smile was radiant. "It looked a lot nicer six hours ago, before we searched the whole city for you."

"You were looking for me?"

"Yeah!" Jude said. "I saw you get into a limousine at the park! We thought you were in trouble!"

"I'm not in trouble at all. See, I took Bristol's advice and asked for a meeting with a reporter. One thing led to another pretty quickly. Apparently, we're bigger celebrities here than we know—the aid workers have been keeping us from the press—I think they're just trying to protect us—but the world knows too little about the USA and they've been wanting to talk to a refugee to get our perspective. I think that's why they're treating you like a rock star."

Bristol nodded. "I got that feeling, too. Like I was from Mars."

"You might as well be. The USA isolated itself so long ago and there have been such a small number of escapees that no one knows what it's really like there; all they have are rumors and press releases, which they know to be untrue."

"But a reporter picked you up in a limo? That still doesn't seem right," Bristol said.

"No, I'm getting to that. The reporter was so excited that I sought him out and wanted to schedule an interview right away, but I thought I'd check with the group to make sure that was okay. Besides Bristol, none of us have talked to the press, and I wanted to be sure I was saying the right things before I just started talking. He was disappointed, but told me to take my time. Then he said that his boss had an interview that day with the First Minister and invited me to come along."

"The First Minister?"

"As in the leader of the government here. The One of Scotland."

Jude's jaw dropped. "What did you say?"

"I said yes, I'd love to tag along, and he said he hoped I'd grant him an exclusive interview this week. I was happy to agree to that."

"That was wise," Jude said while his feet dangled off the floor.

Samara smiled. "I'm glad you think so. So the Secret Service picked me up a few hours later at the park, since the aid organization would be suspicious to see them at Olympic Village, and we all went to St. Andrew's House."

"And you met with the First Minister?" Bristol sounded like he only half-believed her, or maybe he was just that tired.

"Yes, I did. I sat and listened through the interview, and we talked briefly at the end. She didn't have much time to talk in detail, but she had two pieces of advice for us."

Bristol and Jude leaned over their mugs.

"One," Samara said, "we get all the refugees as organized as possible, and try as much as possible to have the same goals."

"That's what I said!" Bristol jolted slightly, and drops of instant coffee spilled onto his fingers.

"Well, the First Minister of Scotland agrees with you."

"What's the second piece of advice?" asked Jude.

Samara closed her eyes for a second to remember the moment. The First Minister had looked so poised, so crisp and put together, but not in the same way the Metrics officials always were; she was softer and more natural and less fearful. "Care for each other. Protect each other. Love each other so radically that sacrifice comes as naturally as our next breath."

The birds made their morning sounds outside under the pink sky. Samara had spent so much time remembering that moment since it happened yesterday that she was ready to connect back to this one; she listened to the breath of Jude and Bristol and they quietly pondered the First Minister's advice. Bristol looked up at her face, and as she looked back, she felt the flame of animation quietly tamper down. No longer was she hyper-aware of how her face looked to Bristol. She only wanted to take him in, look into his eyes, tell him, without words, that she was ready to act on this advice.

"I think," said Jude, "we should start calling meetings of everyone. Maybe get Kareale and Tommy and Danovan involved again, just out of courtesy, and because they can help us organize, especially now that they don't have to use intimidation. And we should share everything we know with everyone."

"Great idea. How about tonight?"

"Let's get to work."

"Excuse me?" An aid worker appeared in the doorway. "Are you Bristol?"

"That's me."

The woman looked extremely uncomfortable. "I have two phone messages for you."

"Okay."

"They might be private."

"You can tell us all. These are two of my best friends," said Bristol. Jude beamed.

"Okay...well, the first is from a woman named Cindy? And she wants you to call her right away?"

Bristol cringed. "Did she seem angry?"

"Well, yes, she did seem a little miffed."

"I'll call her. And the second?"

"The second is from your brother-in-law. Your sister is in the hospital in London."

CHAPTER THIRTY-TWO

IT WAS LUCKY THAT BRISTOL WAS THE ONLY ONE AMONG THEM who had any money at all, thanks to his overnight fame. He didn't have to beg or borrow to pay for three train tickets to London; they'd quibbled a bit about who would go and who would stay, but in the end, Bristol felt better about inviting both Jude and Samara along. As far as he was concerned, the Red Sea and its constant demands could wait. He needed to know that his sister was going to be okay.

On the train, he slept like the dead, waking himself occasionally by choking on a snore. Ordinarily, he'd be mortified by this, but Samara, in the seat next to his, slept with her head back and her mouth hanging open, and that liberated him from having to pretend he was a beautiful dreamer himself.

Bristol awoke to an attendant lightly shaking his shoulder. "Sir? We've arrived."

In the streets, he found London to be one of the most unusual places he'd ever been; though the colors were similar to Edinburgh, and the wide river reminded him of home, the structures themselves just seemed massive, as if the city were built for giants. The people here seemed roughly the same size, though. Samara also walked with her head up, surveying the immense buildings spaced far apart. Only Jude went through the city with his eyes forward, unimpressed by the new sights. Bristol always liked this about Jude; he was not easily distracted.

The hospital staff would only allow Bristol in the room with his sister. He left Jude and Samara in the waiting room with only a television showing a soap opera for distraction. After many wrong turns and a poor choice of elevator, a nurse finally offered to take Bristol to the room.

"Are you Canadian?" the nurse asked, giving Bristol a side-eye. "You sound Canadian."

Bristol didn't have the energy for the truth. "Yep."

"Which part?"

"The cold part."

The nurse scowled but led him until they stopped in front of a wide wooden door. "In there."

Bristol knocked softly. When no one answered, he opened the door slowly.

Denver was in the bed with a tube coming out of her arm. The florescent lights reflected off the all-white bedding, which made her skin look gray. She looked ten years older than the last time he'd seen her. Stephen did, too—he sat on an armchair next to her, but neither of them were talking. They both looked up when Bristol entered, but did not react otherwise.

"Hi," Bristol said softly. "How—" He stopped himself. *How are you?* *Are you insane?* Instead of trying to fix his blunder, he gave Denver a gentle hug around the shoulders.

"I lost the baby," she said. Her voice had a raspy quality to it that seemed to come from deep inside her throat.

"I'm sorry."

"Me too." She moved only her eyes down onto the white blanket covering her lap, keeping even the minuscule muscles of her body still.

"I keep telling her not to say it like that," said Stephen. His eyes were swollen and his cheeks were chapped.

"Like what?" Bristol asked.

"*She* didn't lose the baby. It wasn't her fault."

"It was my job to keep him safe. I couldn't keep him safe."

A red spot blossomed on the blanket tucked under Denver's legs. It was spreading faster than Bristol could react. "Denver..."

"That keeps happening." Stephen pressed the call button on Denver's bed. "She's lost a lot of blood. They keep saying it's not normal."

A nurse came in, flicked her eyes from the blood to some kind of monitor, and immediately got to work changing her sheets. Bristol backed out of the room, though no one had asked him to go. Denver would usually be the first person to tell him to get out if no one else would, but the woman inside wasn't Denver anymore. Some part of her, he feared, had died with her baby. He'd expected some crying, some pain, but not this, not Denver connected to machines and disconnected from everything else.

The baby was a hope, a laugh in the face of the system he'd grown up with. Metrics tried to control when and how and if they could all have children, then restrict how they grew. Force themselves upon the people they'd grow into. Bristol loved knowing that two people in love could simply make a child when they wanted; that was Nature's gift to them. Now, more than ever, he hated Metrics and what they had done to all of them. They had ruined Denver's future all because Bristol existed; they had made her pregnancy fraught with stress and fear; they had encouraged taking responsibility even when the mistake truly wasn't her own.

The nurse walked out with a little nod to him, and he went back inside. He wanted to comfort her somehow, but nothing seemed like the right thing to say. He wanted to tell her that they'd conceive another child, but that gave no comfort for the loss of this one. He himself didn't want *another* niece or nephew, but the one who was already gone. Instead, after several long minutes, he cleared his throat and asked where the baby was.

"He's..." Stephen started to answer, but the words got caught in his throat and he shook his head, as if to say he couldn't speak anymore.

In monotone, Denver said, "He's in the refrigerator in our hotel room. It's our only miracle that's come from all this. The maid who found me knew that the hospital would throw him in the garbage otherwise. She came to the hospital this afternoon and told Stephen she thought we had the right to make the choice about where to lay him."

Bristol's teeth caught his lip.

"Have you thought about where that will be?"

"Yes—"

The door opened before she could tell him, and Samara peeked inside. "They told us we could come up after all if we wanted...can we come in?"

Stephen waved them in. Denver raised her eyebrows at Bristol. "I know it's crazy, but whenever that door opens, I keep thinking it's going to be Mom." For the first time, her voice became jagged and her eyes shut. "I want Mom."

Samara ran over to her bedside and held her arms out. Denver sunk into Samara's breast, her hands still in her lap, her head next to her heart.

CHAPTER THIRTY-THREE

THREE DAYS LATER, ONCE DENVER WAS OUT OF THE HOSPITAL and Stephen had rescheduled the training and the five of them had taken a night train back to Edinburgh, two hundred people spilled onto the sidewalk in front of Daniel's garden. A hole, not wide but deep, gaped under a cherry tree, not far from the ashes of the burned bush. Sitting beside the hole was a small wooden box, painted baby blue. In the unusually sunny early spring sunlight, the box shone on the grass. Denver, Stephen, Bristol, Samara, and Jude sat in chairs that had been dragged out of the house and placed on the brilliant grass. Nearly everyone else stood.

"We gather here," Daniel said to the crowd of refugees and passers-by on the street who'd stopped to listen, "To celebrate the brief but meaningful life of—"

"Zion," said Denver.

"Zion Steiner." Daniel made a wet-sounding sniff and held the handwritten note close to his face. "He was...loved fully...by his parents and his community..." Daniel's nose was nearly touching the paper.

Just before it seemed he would lose his composure completely, there was a rumbling behind the lines of people on the street. The mourners in the garden turned their heads to see what was causing the disruption. Six men in suits and sunglasses walked forward between the crowd. Denver made a motion as if to run for the box, but stopped when the men parted and a woman in a mouse-brown pantsuit stepped through the center.

"I'm sorry to cause a scene," she said to Denver, "but I wanted to come and pay my respects. I'm so sorry for your loss."

Samara gave a little squeak but did not speak. Denver stared speechless at this woman, but the woman didn't seem the least put off. "My name is Cara Clovinger. I am the First Minister of Scotland." She looked at Daniel. "When you're finished, might I give a few words?"

Daniel nodded with wide eyes. "That...that was about all I had."

"Then I'll take it from there." She addressed the little gang in the garden. Cameras hovered now, from news crews that they hadn't noticed before, through the iron bars at the gates. Clara Clovinger cleared her throat. "Though you, Zion's people, have known almost nothing but hardship throughout this year, this little boy knew only love and warmth in his mother's womb. Denver and Stephen Steiner did what any parent would do for their child—fought for his future. Together with their family and friends, they have overcome seemingly insurmountable obstacles in the hope for a better life for him and for all the children born in this community of brave souls. I bring a message of condolence, also, from an ally of yours still in America, known as the Bird. He wants to assure you that he will continue to work for a better world to bring your future children into, and invites you to join him after you've taken all the time you need to grieve your son. I speak for our country when I say we are proud that this boy, with courage in his blood, will be laid to rest in Scottish soil. God rest your soul, little one."

Denver winced as Bristol got up and lowered the box into the hole. She felt softer now than she had ever been before, but she still wouldn't allow herself a breakdown with all these people around. There would be time later to weep in Stephen's arms, both for Zion and for themselves. Although they'd agreed they'd talk it over with the entire community, there was no question now that both of them would go back and be part of the plan to liberate the USA. She could think of no greater gift she could give to Zion, and she had a great need to give him everything she had, even in death.

The First Minister stepped aside, and as Bristol piled fresh earth into the grave, Daniel stood and sang:

Ae fond kiss, and then we sever;
Ae farewell, alas, for ever!
Deep in heart-wrung tears I'll pledge thee,
Warring sighs and groans I'll wage thee
Who shall say that Fortune grieves him
While the star of hope she leaves him?
Me, nae cheerful twinkle lights me,
Dark despair around benights me.

THE END

Thank you for reading!

Please consider leaving a review.

Find book one of the Children of the Uprising,
UNREGISTERED, and discover more from author
Megan Lynch at www.mlynch.net

**Living the ideal life is a human right,
unless you're unregistered.**

Living under the watchful eye of the Metrics Worldwide Government has
its perks. Citizens are assigned a life, so they don't worry about finding
schools, jobs, or spouses for themselves. They're even allowed to have one
child, enabling them to focus on raising an ideal son or daughter and
experience an optimally satisfying family life.

The only people left out are the unlucky accidental second children,
called the unregistered. For 20-year-old Bristol, this is the only life he
knows. But he can't shake the feeling that something is wrong with his
world, and spends his nights painting controversial murals in low-profile
parts of town.

Metrics doesn't like the murals, or the frustrations of the unregistered
citizens they represent.

They enact their long-debated unregistered solution: publicly, they
announce the relocation of all unregistered citizens to far-off desert
states. But when Bristol and his friends discover the dark truth behind
the plan, they must work together to escape the clutches of their
motherland, and survive long enough to discover an unknown world.

Thank you for reading! For more from Megan Lynch, check out her
website and join the mailing list.

Facebook: www.facebook.com/mlriggs

Twitter: www.twitter.com/mlynchbooks

Instagram: www.instagram.com/m.lynch.books/

Website: www.mlynch.net

Please sign up for the City Owl Press newsletter for chances to win special subscriber-only contests and giveaways as well as receiving information on upcoming releases and special excerpts.

All reviews are **welcome** and **appreciated**. Please consider leaving one on your favorite social media and book buying sites.

For books in the world of romance and speculative fiction that embody Innovation, Creativity, and Affordability, check out City Owl Press at www.cityowlpress.com.

ACKNOWLEDGMENTS

To thank everyone who had a hand in this book's birth wouldn't be possible, but there are several incredible people whose influence really needs to be acknowledged.

To Ryan, my husband and best friend, who comforts me when the state of the world and the way humans treat each other gets me down, and who helps me translate that sorrow into stories.

To Finnegan Dean and Clark Francis, who, at this point in their development, couldn't care less that their mother is an author. Thank you, boys, for always showing me what's really important and teaching me organization and focus.

To my family: Mom, Dad, Nanny, Brian, Kevin, Jamie, Rich, Dianne, Lindsay, Tim, Elissa, and Michael. Not one of you ever sprinkled any doubt or discouragement when I said I wanted to write this series. Your encouragement is a big reason this book (and its predecessor) exists.

To the editors and the publishing team: Jennifer Chesak, Amanda Roberts, Melissa Hollingsworth, Tina Moss, and Yelena Casale. Thank the Lord for you people! Truly, I'm thrilled to work with you and I am in awe of your grammatical, structural, and character development skills. Thanks for believing in Bristol, Samara, Denver, and Jude, and making their story shine.

To two of the most interesting people I know, Claire Gilbert and Kevin Clancy. Thanks for living intentionally and holding creativity so close to your hearts. I'm just happy to know you both.

To the readers, especially those who leave reviews. Thanks for taking the time to read and write. I can't think of a better way to spend our days here together.

ABOUT THE AUTHOR

MEGAN LYNCH lives in Nashville, Tennessee with her husband and her sons, Finnegan and Clark. Her debut dystopian novel, Unregistered, depicts the underside of a utopian society when some members live on the fringe and don't fit in. In addition to writing, she loves reading, running, yoga, music, and human rights.

www.mlynch.net

ABOUT THE PUBLISHER

City Owl Press is a cutting edge indie publishing company, bringing the world of romance and speculative fiction to discerning readers.

www.cityowlpress.com